I0612377

WICHITA ARTISTIQUE

WICHITA DETECTIVE
BOOK FOUR

PATRICK ANDREWS

ROUGH
EDGES
PRESS

Wichita Artistique
Paperback Edition
Copyright © 2022 Patrick Andrews

Rough Edges Press
An Imprint of Wolfpack Publishing
9850 S. Maryland Parkway, Suite A-5 #323
Las Vegas, Nevada 89183

roughedgespress.com

Paperback ISBN 978-1-68549-176-5
eBook ISBN 978-1-68549-175-8
LCCN 2022946425

In Memory of
The Boulevard Theater of Yesteryear

WICHITA ARTISTIQUE

"Listen up, Dwayne! Any unwise stunts on your part will prove fatal for both you and Donna Sue!"

– Peter Van Dyke, Art Dealer

CHAPTER 1

It was early evening as Dwayne Wheeler, Wichita private detective, turned off East Central Street into the parking lot of the Dawson Construction Company. He had received a phone call earlier that day informing him that Carl Dawson, the owner of the business, wanted to see him after working hours.

Dwayne pulled up to the plate glass front of the building and could see the figure of a man standing inside, holding the door open. The shamus got out of his car and walked over to the entrance.

"You're Wheeler, right?"

"That's me. I would guess that you're Mister Dawson."

"Yeah. C'mon in."

Dawson led Dwayne past the reception area through a door that opened up on a large room. It was obviously set up for the study of blue prints and drafting. An office kiosk was located in the far corner. That was where the potential client took him.

"Have a seat," Dawson said, going around the desk

and settling down. He opened a drawer and pulled out a 5x7 portrait photograph and handed it to Dwayne. "That's my wife."

Now the shamus knew that this caper would involve one spouse who wanted the other spouse put under surveillance to see if he or she was fooling around. Dwayne studied the image. Middle-age, slightly plump, nice hairdo and plenty of good looks still hanging on after her youth. She didn't seem exactly like the average promiscuous woman, but there was an obvious hint of a sexual persona in the likeness. In most cases this latter characteristic was stimulated when the subject individual felt bored, restless, unappreciated or unloved.

Dwayne looked up, waiting for Dawson to begin speaking.

"I think she's seeing some guy. I want her checked out."

"Right," Dwayne replied, pulling a notebook from an inside jacket pocket. "What time of day do you suspect possible trysts are taking place?"

"During my work hours. That's from the dark of the morning to the dark of the evening. I'm tied down pretty much by the company's operations."

Ah! Then it's prob'ly boredom, Dwayne thought. "Do you have any idea who the guy might be?"

"No."

"Do you have any knowledge regarding where she's meeting the guy?"

"No."

"Okay," Dwayne said. "Here's the best way we can handle a situation like this. And it's simple. I tail her during daylight hours to see when and where she goes. What kind of car does she drive?"

"A '48 Mercury four-door," Dawson said. "Green in

color." He took a business card from his wallet and slid it across the desk. "As soon as you find out anything—anything at all—contact me here at the company number. It'll be answered by my receptionist. Just tell her you are anonymous. Got that? *Anonymous*. She'll know to ring my desk phone. And I've also written down my home address on the back of the card. It's on Mayfair off of East Douglas."

"My rates are twenty-five dollars a day and expenses; which in this case will only be gasoline. I'll need a fifty dollar retainer. Not refundable but applied to the final total of the bill."

"Good enough," he said, reaching into the desk drawer and pulling out a roll of bills. After peeling off five tens, he handed them over. "I guess that's all."

Dwayne nodded, and stood up. "I'll be in touch."

———

THE OFFICE OF THE WHEELER DETECTIVE Agency—newly renamed from Private Investigator, Confidential Service—was located in the Snodgrass Building on West Douglas in downtown Wichita. Dwayne's reason for the new title was to make his small business appear to be a large office with a team of special investigators. It was pure bullshit, but Dwayne figured that made his one-man operation more impressive.

The landlord of the building was Twig Clanton. He was a short, balding skinny man in his thirties who had inherited the property. It was a rundown three-story building with an elevator that had been out of order since the 1930s. He had problems keeping tenants mostly because they moved to classier sites when their businesses became more profitable.

Dwayne and Clanton despised each other with an unending loathing. This was the result of numerous incidents of Clanton locking the detective's office door when he was behind in his rent. Dwayne stayed on only because he didn't spend much time in the office anyway and it seemed like a bad idea to find costlier quarters.

Now, following his hiring by Carl Dawson, Dwayne walked into the lobby of the Snodgrass Building. Twig Clanton was in his favorite worn leather easy chair that had been in the building ten years before the elevator conked out. The landlord was waiting to catch any deadbeat tenants passing by who owed him back rent. He hadn't seen Dwayne for a while. Unknown to the landlord, Dwayne's absence was because of a clandestine undercover assignment for the F.B.I.

"Hey, Wheeler," came the greeting in a surly tone of voice.

"Hey, Clanton," he replied just as coldly.

"Where you been, Wheeler? I ain't seen you for a spell."

"I've been up in Canada."

"Canada? What the fuck was you doing up there?"

"I went there to learn to speak Canadian."

Clanton was puzzled. "Really? Hey! Say something in Canadian."

"Okay," Dwayne said. "On King! On you huskies!"

"That ain't Canadian! That's what Sergeant Preston of the Mounties says at the start of his radio show."

"Well o'course, you dipshit," Dwayne snapped. "He's in the Royal Canadian Mounted Police, ain't he? So anything he says is in Canadian."

Clanton gave him a furious frown. "You're a real asshole, you know that, Wheeler? I bet you don't know a single word in the Canadian language."

"You got me, Clanton. I couldn't fool you."

Clanton settled back in his chair with a satisfied grin as Dwayne walked across the lobby to go upstairs. He went up to his office, letting himself into the small room. He sat down behind the desk and dialed the phone.

A bright feminine voice answered the call. "Reliable Answering Service!"

"Hi, Millie. It's me, Dwayne Wheeler. Any calls?"

"You got one, Dwayne. It came from the Riverview Hotel. The party wants you to call there and ask for Suite 206."

"I have the hotel's number," Dwayne said. "Thanks much." He hung up and dialed the hotel, asking for the suite.

A familiar voice answered. "Is that you, Dwayne?"

"It sure is. So you're back in town, huh, Pete?"

"Yep and Sybil is with me. She says to say 'Hi'."

Peter Van Dyke had been Dwayne's commanding officer in the military police during the war. The pair formed a partnership to deal in Germany's illegal black market at the end of the conflict. Everything went along fine until Dwayne drew attention to himself by living in a large apartment with an extremely attractive and obviously expensive *fräulein*. An inquiry by the Army's Criminal Investigation Division resulted in Dwayne's arrest. The charges against him had been serious, but the U.S. Army didn't want any bad publicity to come out of the incident. The result was a discharge from the U.S. Army for the "convenience of the government." Van Dyke made a subtle withdrawal from the racket and remained in the Army until receiving an honorable release from active duty.

Later after the war, Van Dyke connected with Dwayne in Wichita to take part in a scheme of counterfeiting Nazi military scrip that could be changed into U.S. dollars. This was accomplished by turning it in to the present West German government. The harried bureaucrats hadn't expected phony certificates, and automatically exchanged dollars for the scrip as prescribed by the terms of the unconditional surrender to the Allies.

Dwayne made five thousand dollars in untraceable cash along with a 1941 Buick sedan for services rendered in the scam. That had been the start of his rebound from poverty to a semblance of high living.

"Tell Sybil hi," Dwayne said, remembering her beauty and sexiness. "So what brings you back to good ol' Wichita, Kansas?"

"Art, ol' buddy," Pete said. "I'm talking about valuable paintings." Then he added, "And it's all on the up and up. And you can pull in some big bucks if you accept my offer. This is the type of work that's right up your alley. Sybil and I would like you to come over to the hotel for a dinner from room service this evening. It will be more private than down in the restaurant. Say around seven o'clock."

"Sure," Dwayne said. "But starting tomorrow I'm gonna be busy for the next five or so days on a caper."

"That's no problem. I can give you the lowdown on this art deal."

"I'll be there with bells on," Dwayne promised.

CHAPTER 2

The reunion of Dwayne with Pete and Sybil Van Dyke began with happy greetings when he arrived at the couple's suite. The best part of the salutation for Dwayne was a chance to kiss Sybil on the mouth. It was only a peck, but it was nice to get that close to her. He always thought she had a strong resemblance to Lauren Bacall with her sleepy-eyed beauty, long flowing auburn locks and breasts that defied her svelte body.

Pete Van Dyke had rugged good looks that matched his former background as a wealthy sportsman. But that ended when his father lost the family's fortune during the Great Depression. It resulted in Pete being flung down from the life of a playboy to scrambling for temporary jobs in his hometown of New York City. The problem was a dearth of employment for his qualifications as a polo and tennis player along with an ability in sailing. The best-paying job he got was six weeks being an assistant on a coal truck. He did the unloading.

But when the war started Pete was able to reassume the role of a gentleman when he went into the Army. He qualified for Officers Candidate School and was commissioned a second lieutenant. It was a pseudo-aristocracy but a big leap up from being a poor struggling civilian with no working skills. Unfortunately, after the war ended he still had no real job potential. But before returning to the States he became friends with a rather nefarious upper-class British gentleman by the name of Nigel Hawthorne.

Hawthorne had valuable contacts in the criminal organizations of several European countries. He had been an officer in the British Army but was cashiered for embezzling funds from his regiment's officers mess.

Now he used many aliases and had a forged passport for each one. This helped him to be a complete unknown to all the military and police intelligence agencies in Europe. He was also fluent in the French and German languages.

Hawthorne met Pete Van Dyke through his black market activities. The two recognized each other as kindred souls and the Englishman brought Pete into several of his profitable racketeering organizations.

———

NOW IN THE RIVERVIEW HOTEL, DWAYNE, PETE, and Sybil had a short and sweet happy hour. The two men imbibed scotch while Sybil enjoyed her usual vodka tonics. The couple had lately participated in various financial activities in France arranged by Nigel Hawthorne. The swindle had continued unabated until the truth of some of the seedier deals leaked out. Pete and the Englishman, as usual, made smooth escapes unnoticed by local authorities or Interpol.

After everyone had a buzz on, Pete called down to

room service and ordered the best steak dinners offered by the exclusive hotel for him and Dwayne. Sybil, vain about her willowy figure, had the baked chicken special and a garden salad.

An hour later, with the effects of the liquor dulled by the heavy meals, they settled down for the evening's discussion. Pete Van Dyke began by saying, "The first thing I want to let you in on, is that Nigel Hawthorne is running this show. I'm sure you remember him from the German military scrip job."

"Sure," Dwayne replied. "I met him out in the Chicago suburbs when I made deliveries of the plates. He ran a slick operation with that scrip. So what's his latest scheme?"

"This new deal is all about very expensive paintings. And—I'm not lying—it's all honest but not exactly above board."

Dwayne took a sip of scotch. "That's pretty confusing."

"Strange but true. There is a cabal of extremely wealthy art collectors who have the means and money of selling and buying great works of art. As near as I can figure, there's probably a dozen or so of 'em scattered around the world. The under-the-table aspect is the secrecy maintained among the members of the group."

Dwayne frowned. "I still don't get it."

"Instead of displaying their collections openly in museums or galleries, they all have basement show rooms with climate control," Pete explained. "The only people they allow in those areas are fellow members."

Sybil interjected, "I personally think it's a stingy arrangement. They don't want any common folks to enjoy the work of some of the greatest artists in the world."

"I understand now," Dwayne said. "But where do I come in?"

"They buy their art from each other and also from dealers who like the inflated prices they're willing to pay," Pete said. "At this moment in their dealings they find it convenient to put some of the more expensive works in storage. The time out of circulation will increase the already considerable value of the art. There is going to be some rather sensitive shipping done in those transactions. What is needed is a central place to hold these master-pieces. Obviously this has to be in an isolated location. And Wichita fits the bill perfectly."

"I get it," Dwayne acknowledged. "I'm the guy who will receive those secret shipments."

"Right," Pete said. "And you're also the guy who eventually will ship them off to their final destinations once you have the clearance to do so."

"Sounds great," Dwayne commented. "But it's gonna be awkward dealing with paintings, isn't it?"

"They're not in their frames. The art is rolled up like wallpaper in thick cardboard tubes."

"Okay. So where do I keep 'em?"

"There's a very secure and virtually unknown rental vault company right here in Wichita," Pete informed him. "I've checked it out and they offer 36-inch high by 48-inch long by 48-inch wide strongboxes. I've already reserved one for you. We can go down and sign for it as soon as you're able."

"Okay," Dwayne agreed. "I get a tube mailed to me and I take it down to the vault. Later on I'll get instructions on where to mail it, I take it out and send it along."

"It's all by registered mail. That leaves a record of the packages' comings and goings, but the receivers have the means to make that information disappear. This can be done easily because of the wealth and connections of the art collectors. Sweet, huh?"

"Well, the next thing I need to know now is how much do I get paid."

"You'll be put on a salary," Pete told him. "Two hundred bucks a week."

Dwayne's jaw dropped. "Say again!"

Pete grinned. "I say again. Two hundred dollars and I'll be your contact man."

"I definitely want in on this," Dwayne assured him. "But right now I'm obligated on a caper. But I can report for duty next Tuesday after wrapping things up for my client."

"That's fine," Pete said. "I'll send a wire to Nigel Hawthorne. He'll be happy to learn you've accepted the offer."

Sybil smiled. "Well! I think this is wonderful! And I could use another drink."

"I can take care of that," Pete said. He got up and walked over to the sideboard. "Vodka tonic for the lady and scotch whiskey neat for the gentlemen."

CHAPTER 3

Dwayne Wheeler began his caper for Carl Dawson the next morning by parking at the corner of East Douglas and Mayfair. He arrived at the spot a little after eight a.m. The shamus lit a Lucky Strike and began a period of smoking and waiting.

He had a lunch box containing a sandwich and miscellaneous snacks. There was also a thermos of water for sipping to keep his thirst down. He would have brought coffee, but on this kind of caper it would mean having to take numerous piss breaks that would interrupt the investigation. Dwayne always had a large fruit jar with a lid for unexpected urinating but using it was awkward and, in some cases, impossible.

He was about to light up another Lucky when the Mercury sedan appeared and halted at the stop sign on Douglas. He could see a woman in the car and followed her after she made a left turn. The traffic was light and he was able to allow cars to get between him and Mrs. Dawson and still keep her from noticing she was being tailed.

They continued down Douglas to Hillside and she made another left turn. A few more minutes of driving and she executed a right turn onto Harry Street. After a short jaunt, Mrs. Dawson turned right on Schweiter Drive then made a left onto Aloma into a middle class neighborhood.

She pulled over and parked in the middle of the block. Dwayne went past, glad to see there were a number of cars parked on the street so he wouldn't stand out when pulling up to the curb. He noted the residence she was walking toward in the rear view mirror and made a U-turn to a spot where he could keep the dwelling under surveillance. By using his binoculars, he could see the number on the house she visited.

Mrs. Dawson stayed inside the residence just short of a couple of hours. When she emerged to go back to the Mercury sedan, she was accompanied by a lady who appeared to be her age. They talked for a couple of minutes, then exchanged hugs. Mrs. Dawson got into her car and headed back to Harry Street.

She went straight home and Dwayne took up his viewing position once more at the corner of Douglas and Mayfair. After a couple of hours, he sensed the lady would not be going out again, and he headed downtown. The first thing he did when he arrived was to make a phone call to the Sedgwick County Clerk's office. He requested the name of the person or persons living at the house on Aloma Drive. It was a Miss Lila Lynton and she was the only resident dwelling there.

THE ROUTINE WAS THE SAME THE NEXT DAY. Once again she stayed for about two hours and her lady friend accompanied her back to the car and they parted after a friendly hug. What the shamus observed gave no indication of a man being involved in the visit. Dwayne began to think that Carl Dawson was one of those control-freak husbands who didn't want their wives to have any friends outside their home.

A change in the routine came on Friday morning. Mrs. Dawson carried a small suitcase into the house. Four hours later Dwayne noticed one of the neighbors was standing on his front porch eyeing him. The guy had probably noticed his presence and was getting curious. Dwayne took out his notebook and faked writing in it to give the impression he was conducting some sort of business in the area. Then he drove away.

He came back several times Saturday and Mrs. Dawson's car had not been moved. Just for drill he returned at three a.m. Sunday morning. The Mercury was still parked in the same spot. He made several more drive-bys all through that day and it was obvious Mrs. Dawson was still inside the dwelling. But when he came back on Monday morning her car was gone. Dwayne drove to her house on Mayfair Street and sighted the vehicle in the driveway.

Dwayne went to his office to type up a report and an invoice to present to Dawson. He began composing the details of his investigation on the second-hand Remington portable that he'd lately purchased in a pawn shop. With that done, he took out his client's business card and dialed the phone number. A feminine voice answered, saying, "Dawson Construction."

"Hi," Dwayne said. "I'm Anonymous. I'd like to speak to Mister Dawson."

"Thank you, sir," the female replied.

Dwayne thought there was something familiar about

the voice, but quickly put it out of his mind when Dawson came on the line. "You got any info for me, Wheeler?"

"Yeah, Mister Dawson. I—"

"Okay," the man interrupted. "I'm gonna have to be out of the office for the next half hour or so. How about driving over here? We can have a talk."

"Can do," Dwayne replied. "I'll bring a typed report and my invoice."

Dwayne gathered his paperwork and left the office. He was in a hurry to wind up the caper so he could start earning the two hundred bucks a week working with Pete Van Dyke. It only took him twenty minutes to get over to Dawson's place of business. He parked in a visitor's spot, then got out and walked into the lobby up to the receptionist's desk.

"My God!" he exclaimed.

Donna Sue Connors, his old flame, looked up at him. "Why Dwayne!"

The last thing he knew about Donna Sue was that she was in a romantic and sexual relationship with Brian Murchison, a petroleum engineering executive. The guy was the scion of one of Wichita's wealthiest families. The affair came about after she tired of slinging hash in the Jayhawker Restaurant in downtown Wichita. At that time, she and Dwayne were an item. She took night classes and received a high school graduate equivalency certificate so she could enroll in secretarial school. That led to a job at Murchison Enterprises where she became the boss's girlfriend. Dwayne was left out in the cold.

"So you're the receptionist here? What happened to your secretary job? Are you still seeing Brian Murchison?"

"He's married."

"Wow! Were you expecting that?"

Donna shook her head. "His wife is the daughter of a petroleum high roller in Houston, Texas. He wanted me to be his mistress and offered to put me up in an apartment. The bastard promised to support me."

Dwayne knew she would have been insulted by the suggestion. "You turned him down, didn't you?"

"Yes, and I was fired. It's that simple."

"That don't sound simple to me." Dwayne could see he was about to pull one of his *faux pas* as usual with a woman. He decided to switch moods. "Would you like to have dinner with me this evening? We could bring ourselves up to date with one another. Remember the Stockyards Hotel Restaurant?"

"Well...sure! I'd love to go."

"I'll make a reservation. Where do you live?"

"In the 500 block of North Erie Avenue," she replied. "There's an apartment building on the corner."

"Well that's handy, A short drive, huh?"

"I take the bus. I lost the company car when I was kicked out of Murchison Enterprises. I'm in Apartment 325."

The glass front door opened and Carl Dawson walked in, gesturing at Dwayne to follow him. The shamus hurried after his client. When they got into his office, Dawson sat down behind his desk. "Okay. Give it to me."

"Actually, I got good news, Mister Dawson," Dwayne began. "Your wife ain't seeing another man. She's visiting another woman. The other lady's name is Lila Lynton."

"Lila?"

"D'you know her?"

"Yeah," Dawson replied. "She's a member of our church."

"Well, I'd say she and your wife are good friends. Fact is, Missus Dawson spent the weekend with her."

"*What*?"

"You seem surprised," Dwayne said. "Didn't you know about it?"

"My wife told me she was going to visit her mother in Hutchinson."

Dwayne shook his head. "She showed up at Lila Lynton's house and stayed there from Saturday 'til Monday morning. I even went back at three a.m. on Sunday and her Mercury was still parked in front."

Dawson was visibly shaken. "Why in hell would she lie about *that*?"

"I can't help you there," Dwayne said. "Here's my report and my invoice. It comes to a hunnerd and fifty bucks. I didn't charge for gas since it didn't amount to much."

Dawson reached into a side desk drawer, getting some bills. He counted out the required amount. "Can you keep my name off your books?"

Dwayne was used to clients wanting to stay unlisted and anonymous. "The law allows me the right to refuse to reveal your name or anything else about you. You'll be listed as a case number."

Dwayne left the office, walked across the drafting room and out into the lobby. He stopped at Donna Sue's desk. "You want a ride home? I can come back and pick you up."

"Yes, thanks, Dwayne. I get off at five o'clock."

CHAPTER 4

Dwayne didn't go back to his office after leaving Dawson Construction. The unexpected meeting with Donna Sue had actually shook him up quite a bit. He'd managed to keep a lid on his feelings after their breakup. Now he wanted to be alone for some deep consideration of this new situation.

His mind was so occupied from seeing her again that he ran a red light. It didn't cause an accident, but he elicited angry honks from other motorists. He forced himself to be extra attentive as he continued on his way to his residence on Market Street.

Dwayne found a parking place in front of the apartment house and sat in the car for a few minutes as waves of sentiment held him motionless. It was a surreal moment that was both perplexing and upsetting. After a few minutes the sensations settled down enough for him to get out of the car and go inside.

After entering his apartment, Dwayne suddenly became light headed to the point he was afraid he might actually faint. The shamus crossed slowly over to the bedroom door and sat down on the bed, leaning back against the headboard. He took several deep breaths to recover from the disquieting anxiety.

"Damn! This is really shitty!" he exclaimed out loud. "I feel like somebody hit me up the side of the head with a baseball bat."

It was only a few short weeks ago that he'd been forced to face the realization that he was still in love with Donna Sue. That knowledge had upset him, but not quite as bad as on this particular day. He had known she was happy in her relationship with Brian Murchison and he pushed her as far back into the recesses of his mind as possible.

Now in less than an hour all that had changed.

He suddenly experienced a fresh joyful surge that he might be able to rekindle their romance. Then that joyful surge plummeted to a heartrending nose-dive. Murchison had more than likely taken her on trips to Europe's finest attractions in Paris, London, Madrid and a dozen other places. She'd undoubtedly met other men during those excursions and many of them would be wealthy playboy bachelors who would come seeking her out after hearing about the present situation.

Dwayne was painfully aware he was presently facing another anguishing heartbreak. He felt like getting blind drunk, but there was the dinner date for that evening. He got off the bed and began disrobing to take a bath and shave.

THE STOCKYARDS HOTEL RESTAURANT SOUNDED like a cheap dump to the uninitiated but in truth, it was a high class place with an impeccable cuisine that included the finest steak dinners. The nearby stockyards were involved in commercial transactions of hundreds of thousands of dollars. The ranchers and purchasing agents conducting business there came from all over the West and Midwest. They may have been a bit crude and rustic, but that collective appearance belied their financial worth.

Their favorite thing to do when they had some time off was to go to Las Vegas. The high rollers were given free accommodations in the casinos and like most gamblers they bet and lost heavily. Even though their losses were in the thousands of dollars, it didn't bother them. They returned to their mansions, private airplanes and luxury boats completely undisturbed. The big bucks rolling in from the ranching and meatpacking enterprises they owned always replenished their coffers.

———

Dwayne had managed to settle down a bit as he arrived in the parking lot of Dawson Construction at a quarter to five. He found a spot where he was close enough to watch the front door. Twenty minutes later several women emerged. Dwayne rightly assumed they were all administrative assistants such as secretaries and stenographers. He figured Donna Sue was hired as a receptionist because of her classy good looks.

Then she appeared.

Dwayne's anxiety erupted once more during the few moments he had to study her as she walked toward the car. When Donna Sue worked at the Jayhawker Restaurant in downtown Wichita, she was what he considered country girl pretty with blond hair, green eyes, and light freckles. At that moment he appreciated what the exposure to posh people had done for her. Although Donna Sue was five years older than he, the woman had become savvy enough in fashion and makeup that she didn't show her age.

Donna Sue, obviously unable to see him, stopped and looked around. He got out of his car and waved. She laughed as she walked over. "I was looking for that old Pontiac."

"I got rid of it a long time ago," he said, opening the passenger door. The '41 Buick was more stylish than the '35 Pontiac Coupe, but he knew she'd no doubt been riding around in fancy sedans built and sold after the war. Cadillacs, Chrysler Windsors, Lincoln Cosmopolitans and others would have been more her modes of transportation.

Donna Sue gave him a quick studied look. "You've changed a lot, Dwayne. I mean for the better. You're kind of chic now."

That comment surprised him. He awkwardly replied, "Well...I...uh...I've been more careful with my money lately. Saved some up for clothes and stuff. And I cut back betting on the ponies."

She laughed. "Oh! I remember those days!"

"I made reservations for six-thirty at the restaurant," Dwayne said. "I hope that's all right."

"It's fine. That gives me plenty of time to powder my nose and change dresses."

She got into the car and Dwayne walked around to the driver's side. When he drove out of the parking lot he shot a quick glance at her. She gave him a warm smile that put him in a very good mood.

When they pulled up in front of her apartment house, Dwayne noted the place was not a particularly impressive building. It was a four-story brick structure that appeared to have been built in the 1920s or earlier. When they went inside he saw that the hallways could use some fresh paint and the carpets were badly worn. They climbed the stairs to the third floor and went down to apartment 325. Donna Sue unlocked the door and led the way inside.

Dwayne was surprised that her rented furniture was so cheap. Perhaps she had really taken a tumble from her obviously infuriated boyfriend. The shamus wouldn't put it past the guy to take back expensive presents he had given her. Rich guys don't like being refused what they want, especially from women.

"I'll be as quick as I can," Donna Sue promised.

"Take your time."

He sat down on the sofa and glanced around. The kitchen was no more than a counter in the corner with a stove, sink and refrigerator behind it. A single door across the apartment obviously opened up to the bedroom and bathroom.

Donna Sue was true to her word and reappeared in twenty minutes after redoing her makeup and changing into a dress and shoes. "You look nice," Dwayne said, liking what he saw.

"Thank you, sir," she cheerfully replied.

They left the apartment and Dwayne was tempted to take her hand as they went down the stairs, but thought it was too early in the reunion. He wanted to proceed carefully with the realization that only self-confidence and patience would win her back. He tried to be positive about his romantic efforts, but he knew the odds were stacked against him.

———

THE MAÎTRE D' AT THE STOCKYARDS HOTEL Restaurant seated the couple at a corner table. When the waiter approached them Dwayne wisely let Donna Sue choose the before dinner drinks and she asked for the Pascal Pinot Noir. When the waiter returned with the wine, he began the usual service routine. Dwayne had seen a lot of that in the movies and he knew enough to slosh it around, stick his nose in the glass and sniff, then take a sip.

"This is fine," he announced. With that done, he told the server they would need a little time to figure out what they wanted off the menu.

He and Donna Sue were both slightly uneasy at first but the conversation segued into their old familiarity. Dwayne tried to stay away from her present circumstances, and she sensed his hesitancy.

"I would like to tell you exactly what happened to me, Dwayne."

"Okay," he mumbled. This did not exactly please him and he began to feel the evening might turn sour.

"Brian Murchison hired me into the company as chief of correspondence with the oil teams out in the field," she explained. "My job was to record their messages in a log, then see that the documents were distributed to the appropriate people."

"That sounds like a pretty important job."

"That's what I thought. At first."

"I see."

"Let me continue my tale of woe," Donna Sue said. "The first thing Brian required from me before I had even started work was not to use my given name of Donna Sue. Just Donna. Brian thought the 'Sue' made it too redneck. Then I was furnished with the first and last month's rent on a fancy place in the Royal Arms Apartments."

"That's in a luxury neighborhood!"

"Fortunately, I was being paid a hefty salary. But I should've known there would be a catch to it somewhere down the line. I learned after the break-up that most of the people in the company considered me a courtesan."

"What's that?"

"A kept woman," she said, taking a sip from her glass. "I'm going to be very revealing now."

Dwayne grimaced inwardly.

"Brian and I had a romantic affair. But I guess you had figured that out by now."

That hurt. "Uh...yeah." Now Dwayne's mind played a dirty trick on him and created a mental picture of her in bed with Murchison. The son of a bitch was between her legs humping away.

Donna Sue continued, "I thought I might be heading for a marriage into a wealthy family. We partied and went to the best places for nights out on the town. But they were all in Wichita. I was so stupid I didn't realize he had women in other cities."

Now Dwayne knew she hadn't been taken to grand venues in Europe. At that time the waiter returned. Donna Sue ordered the ladies' special with the house salad, filet mignon, and roasted vegetables. He chose a 12-ounce T-bone steak with a baked potato, no vegetables and extra rolls. Since Donna Sue would have her salad served first he decided to settle for a Caesar's salad so she wouldn't have to eat alone before the main courses were served.

The waiter departed and Donna Sue said, "I saw those articles on you in the newspapers. It sounded like someone was out to get you."

"Yeah. I'm afraid that's something I can't talk about." He shrugged apologetically. "My detective work has grown more sophisticated over the months."

"Well then, can you tell me how you're getting along with that woman I met in the Roadhouse?"

"We broke up," Dwayne said. "It just wasn't working out."

"I'm sorry to hear that."

The remark disturbed him. It sounded to him like she wasn't interested in restarting their own affair. He wanted to change the subject. "Do you remember when we brought Tommy Brady and Missus Durham here to see if they'd hit it off?"

"Oh, yeah!" she said. "He was the little Salvation Army guy who was a widower and she was the widow of that bookmaker guy whose murder you solved. They were so friendly at first that I was sure we had a romance stirred up there."

"I'm afraid Tommy was still too much in love with his Margie to ever want another woman," Dwayne commented. "I've seen him quite a few times since then. He's real happy at his farm over by Augusta."

"By the way, you're not still living in that boarding house, are you?"

He shook his head. "Nope. I moved out. The landlady Mrs. Busch didn't say goodbye to me, she said good *riddance*!"

Donna Sue laughed. "I'm not surprised. I can remember how you were perpetually behind with your rent."

"Don't forget my troubles with Twig Canton about my office."

They were interrupted by the arrival of their salads, and the conversation died down slightly. Fifteen minutes later the main courses were served and both settled in for some serious dining.

Donna Sue looked up at him from her small steak. "Let's talk about you, Dwayne. What's going on?"

At that moment Dwayne knew this was a great opportunity to pitch himself. "I'm well off," he answered. "In fact, I'm living high. There's been some capers that have brought in big bucks. Thousands all told. I have a nice apartment downtown on Market Street a few blocks south of Douglas." He paused for effect. "Donna Sue, I'm in the chips."

"Good Lord! You're certainly not the old Dwayne Wheeler, are you?"

He could see she was interested and it was a good opportunity to launch a serious campaign. "I've just been hired into a deal that will pay me two hunnerd bucks a week for quite awhile."

"Oh, Dwayne! That's wonderful! What are you doing?"

"It's a caper. That's all I can say." He cleared his throat, swallowed some wine and said, "Speaking of the Roadhouse would you like to go there with me Saturday night?"

"I would love to," she replied.

"Okay, we'll surprise ever'body when we show up together."

"Wait a minute," she said.

His mood sunk. He was sure she had other plans that had slipped her mind.

"I think we should go out to Western Danceland like we used to. It'd be a real kick."

Dwayne was surprised and delighted. "Western Danceland it is!"

This showed Donna Sue had some happy memories of their times together after all.

CHAPTER 5

Dwayne and Pete Van Dyke arrived at Secure Vault Rentals, Incorporated in north Wichita to keep a ten o'clock appointment. They were sent to manager Lawrence Gorcey's office to have him take them through the routine of signing an agreement to use the facilities. After Pete handed over a certified check, they were each given a key.

The next step in the arrangement began when Gorcey escorted them into the interior of the building to one of a half-dozen rooms designated as clientele chambers. This was where the strongbox would be brought out to Dwayne when he needed it. An employee of the company would put a master key in one lock and the shamus in the other to open it. At that point the escort would leave and Dwayne would have complete and secret access to the container.

The manager left them in the chamber to go retrieve the strongbox they had rented. His return amazed Dwayne at the size of the container. It was larger than he had expected and also had wheels. He looked over at Pete.

"When you said 36-inches high by 48-inches long by 48-inches wide, I didn't realize how big that really was."

"It's big all right," Pete agreed. "I should have described it as three feet high by four feet long by four feet wide. It's got to be large since there will be times when you'll store several shipments as well as large packages in it."

"Let's open it, shall we?" Gorcey suggested.

He inserted the company key into a lock on the left side, turning it. This was followed by Dwayne doing the same thing with his key on the right. The manager stated, "If you have anything to put in it now, I'll withdraw."

"Not today," Pete said.

"Very well," Gorcey replied. "Now grasp the handle and turn it clockwise then pull upward."

Dwayne did as he was instructed and lifted the heavy lid. "It looks big enough to put my apartment furniture in there," he joked.

"I assume that's your approval of the device," Gorcey remarked. "I'll be back shortly." He closed the lid and wheeled the strongbox out of the private room. A couple of minutes later their escort returned and led them to the reception area at the front of the building. After a quick parting from Gorcey, they went to Pete's rental Lincoln sedan to return to the Riverside Hotel.

———

SYBIL LOOKED UP AS THEY WALKED INTO THE suite. "Is it all set?"

"It sure is," Pete replied. "And now I can give our pal Dwayne a complete briefing on what he'll be doing for the cabal."

"I'm all ears," Dwayne told him.

Sybil asked, "Are you guys thirsty? I can perform some bartender duties before you get started. Or we can have soft drinks from the refrigerator."

"A soft drink for me," Pete said. "It's a little early for me to start imbibing alcohol."

"Me, too," Dwayne commented.

Sybil smiled at the shamus. "And do we have a surprise for you!"

She came back with two bottles of Coca-Cola and a six-pack carton. "We had a bellboy go out and get this for you, Dwayne." She showed him Orange Crush soda pops in a cardboard container.

Dwayne laughed out loud. "All this and two hunnerd bucks a week! I must've died and gone to heaven."

"We aim to please," Pete said. "Now let's get down to business."

Dwayne took a deep swig of his beloved Orange Crush and sat down on the sofa with Sybil. Pete settled into a plush easy chair across from them.

"Okay, pal. Here's how this is gonna work. The items —and that is how the paintings are referred to—will be sent to the special delivery pick-up window at the downtown post office here in Wichita. The postal people will call you when an item arrives and you will go there to sign for them. And do it as quickly as you can after being notified."

"Wilco," Dwayne stated in the Army radio commo way of saying "will comply."

"You are to take the item or items from the post office over to Secure Vault Rental Incorporated and put 'em in our rented strongbox. And again you must do this immediately. Do not let anything delay you in the procedure. Your total concentration must be on the task."

"Wilco."

"And one more thing," Pete said, continuing his instructions. "You must be armed at all times. We don't expect any robbery attempts, but don't take any chances."

"And I say yet again, 'wilco'."

"Each of the items are numbered and you will be informed of when and where you will ship them when the time is right."

"How will I know when the time is right?"

"I will notify you personally," Pete answered. "Sybil and I are going to be back east. I'll give you our business card in a few minutes. I'll also hand over some batches of mailing labels with different addresses. When you mail an item put the proper label on the package, then go to the post office and send it by registered mail to its designated destination."

"That's an easy procedure," Dwayne said. "I can't see any reason why things will not go smoothly on this end."

"Good," Pete said. "And I will be sending you four one hundred dollar money orders every two weeks. I assume you are aware that individual money orders cannot be for more than 100 dollars. That's why you'll be getting four of 'em."

"Yeah, I'm aware of that," Dwayne assured him. "Y'know, I can't see any reason to do a lot of private eye work as long as that amount of money is rolling in."

"Right," Pete agreed. "That is exactly what the powers-that-be want you to do. So concentrate on giving the majority of your time to receiving and sending the mailings." He motioned to Sybil. "Sweetie, fetch one of our business cards for him please." Sybil got up and Pete continued, "We've rented a brownstone on the upper west side in Manhattan."

"New York City, right?"

Sybil returned with a business card and two money orders. "Here you are, Dwayne."

Dwayne grinned. "I gotta say it don't get no better than this!"

"Now let's turn our attention from sodas to scotch," Pete suggested.

———

DWAYNE APPEARED AT DONNA SUE'S APARTMENT in the early evening of the next Saturday. When she responded to the doorbell it was all he could do to keep from giving her a kiss and a tight embrace. Instead he showed a smile as he stepped through the door. "All set for a wild night at Western Danceland?"

"You betchum, Red Ryder," Donna Sue replied, imitating the Indian boy Little Beaver in the *Red Ryder* comic books.

They were dressed appropriately for their evening's destination. Dwayne wore his old fedora hat, an open collar shirt, casual slacks and a sport coat with rodeo pockets and shoulder patches. Donna Sue was clad in a sweater, wide skirt and high heels. She carried a small purse with nothing more in it than some makeup for touch-ups during the evening.

The couple went downstairs to the street and Dwayne continued to be a gentleman by opening the passenger door for her. With his date situated in the car, he got in behind the wheel and headed for South Broadway.

Donna Sue smiled. "It seems strange not to be going there in your old Pontiac."

"Oh, I meant to tell you, my dear," Dwayne said in a comical high-tone voice and accent of a rich snob. "I'm going to be buying a new car. A *brand* new car. Actually not a car. A station wagon. A Nash station wagon."

"Those are expensive, Dwayne!"

"I told you I was in the chips."

He continued driving, feeling smug and sure of himself and happily looking forward to holding Donna Sue while they danced.

———

WESTERN DANCELAND WAS LOCATED A COUPLE of miles south of Wichita on U.S. Highway 81. When Dwayne pulled into the parking lot it was beginning to fill up. There were a dozen or so paint-faded pick-up trucks and older model cars of those early arrivals. Although the vehicles' collective external appearances were tacky, the engines ran smoothly under the expert care of their redneck owners. What those guys lacked in education they made up with skills as mechanics.

Dwayne found a parking place in the back. "I wonder how many fights there's gonna be out here before the night's over."

"Let 's hope none of 'em involve guns," Donna Sue stated seriously. "Or knives."

"Don't count on it."

They walked around the building to the front door and were happily greeted by Benny Gordon the bouncer. He was an ex-paratrooper who had worked with Dwayne on bill collection capers that required punching up errant deadbeats. The pair's clients were mostly bookmakers although there was also the occasional loan shark. Dwayne and Benny were both experts in the use of brass knuckles.

"Are you two together again?" Benny asked with a big grin.

"We're good pals," Dwayne said.

"I just remembered," Benny remarked. "Jesse said if you ever showed up he wants to see you."

Dwayne nodded. "We might as well take care of that matter right away."

He and Donna Sue went inside and walked past the bar to the owner's office. He rapped on the door and it was opened by Jesse's wife Lorene. "Oh! Hello, Dwayne," she greeted. "Come in." She nodded to Donna Sue.

Jesse Pickens, proprietor of the nightclub, looked up from his desk. "Hi, Dwayne." He noticed Donna Sue. "Don't we know you?"

Lorene spoke up. "It's his girlfriend, Jesse. They ain't be in for a spell."

"Oh, yeah. Anyhow, we got something to tell you, Dwayne."

Donna Sue felt like an intruder. "I can wait outside."

"It's okay," Lorene said. She turned her attention to Dwayne. "We wanted to tell you that we lost Mary Sue."

Dwayne knew all about the death of her daughter. She had been a chronic runaway, traveling with truck drivers. Dwayne was also aware that she had sunk into being a prostitute and drug addict. He had been in an F.B.I. undercover caper in which he buried her after an overdose of heroin. It was something he could not reveal to her parents or anyone else.

The shamus cleared his throat. "I saw the obituary. I'm awful sorry."

"It was terrible for us," Lorene said, beginning to sob. "She'd been dug up out of a grave. They told us she was wrapped in a blanket. We wanted to look at her, but the cops said we'd be better off if we didn't. There wasn't nothing left but hair and bones."

Jessie interjected, "The county sent a deputy over to

inform us. They'd learned about it from the Kansas Bureau of Investigation. They had a ring that had been on her finger. It was one we gave her for her birthday last year. And they showed us her shoes, too. They was all covered with dirt."

"The deputy said she was nothing but a skeleton inside a dress," Lorene murmured. "Dwayne, we'll always be grateful to you for the time you found her after she ran away and brung her back to us."

"I'm glad I was able to be of help."

"We tried to get ahold of you when she took off this last time," Jesse stated. "But we couldn't find you."

"I had an out-of-town caper," Dwayne explained. "I wish I could have been here in Wichita and could have found her before...well...before the end."

"Anyhow," Jesse said, "you two go on out there and have a good time."

Dwayne and Donna Sue left the office and found an empty booth where they sat on the same side like they used to. "Well!" Donna Sue said. "That was a downer."

"Yeah," Dwayne agreed. "The Pickens family are their own worst enemies."

A waitress quickly appeared and Dwayne ordered two bottles of Schlitz beer. Donna Sue looked around. "This place hasn't changed a bit."

The interior was dominated on one side by a long, scarred bar where the patrons sat on scuffed wooden stools. A line of battered booths stood along the opposite wall and there was a large dance area in the middle.

"The customers look the same, too," Dwayne said. The raucous crowd's manner of dress ranged from Stetson hats, flowery western-style shirts, jeans and cowboy boots to work clothing.

A half hour passed before the band arrived and immediately went to the stage to set up their instruments. As they went about the chore, Benny Gordon went up and pulled a heavy-gauge steel screen across the stage. This barrier was needed when objects such as beer bottles were thrown at the musicians. This happened when unruly drunks didn't like the way the band was playing their favorite songs.

When the music started, Dwayne and Donna Sue joined the throng on the dance floor and began an enjoyable but wary evening. As time passed a lot of activity besides tripping the light fantastic occurred.

Two women got into a shrieking fight of punching, scratching and kicking. A drunk threw bottles at the band while an angry man stormed into the building and punched a guy who was with his wife. Then he grabbed the woman and dragged her out the door by her hair. Benny the bouncer ejected a total of four troublemakers.

Then after eleven p.m. things really got boisterous.

————

IT WAS ONE O'CLOCK A.M. WHEN DWAYNE PULLED up in front of Donna Sue's apartment house. They were both a little drunk and in a good mood. Dwayne was a bit unsteady on his feet as he walked around the car to open the door for her.

She got out and stretched. "Dancing is good exercise. Hey, care for a nightcap? I have a bottle of scotch in my cupboard."

"Yeah. I would be real happy about having a nightcap."

They walked hand-in-hand to the door of the building and held onto each other as they went up to the third floor. They entered the apartment and Donna Sue

went to the kitchen cabinet to get the scotch while
Dwayne went to the bathroom.

When he returned they settled down on the sofa.
Dwayne had his drink on the rocks and Donna Sue sipped
a glass of chardonnay. He suddenly laughed. "Remember
when you lived in that apartment house where Mister and
Missus Greeley was the landlords?"

"They were a nice old couple," Donna Sue said.
"Their only drawback was that they were too religious.
They didn't allow us women renters to have male visitors
after nine o'clock."

"Yeah. But we beat that rule by having sex *before* we
went out."

"So did everybody else in the place."

Dwayne took another swallow of straight scotch. He
sat the glass down on the coffee table and impetuously
slipped an arm around Donna Sue's shoulders and drew
her to him. He started to stop, then saw she was looking
up at him instead of resisting.

The kiss was moments long and passionate. Then,
almost as by instinct, they got off the sofa and went into
the bedroom.

CHAPTER 6

The small city of Sommerfeld was located in the American Sector of occupied West Germany in the days shortly after World War II. The infrastructure damage the city suffered during the war was mostly cleaned up, repaired and functional. Now its citizens were desperately trying to begin new lives after enduring the overwhelming defeat inflicted upon their country.

They had also lived under the brutality of a cruel dictator who drove them into that horror as he issued orders for their fathers, brothers, and other male relatives to fight to their last bullet. *Nicht Übergabe*—No Surrender!

———

A WEST GERMAN POLICE VOLKSWAGEN ROLLED into the most upscale neighborhood of Sommerfeld. The occupants of the vehicle were a policeman driver and a German Jewish man by the name of David Arnsteiner.

They turned onto Ulme Strasse and came to a stop at

the last house on the street. It was an impressive two-story residence that had gotten through the late conflict without receiving as much as a broken window.

Arnsteiner got out of the car and looked up at the dwelling. He felt a quiver of combined anger and grief for an instant, then fought it down as he always did. He glanced over at the policeman. "Do you have the proper papers?"

The man held up a folder. "Everything is here, *Herr* Arnsteiner. All correct and legal."

They went up to the house and the policeman pushed the doorbell. It was answered by a maid wearing a domestic's dress complete with an ecru net serving cap. The sight of a uniformed *polizist* startled her as it would anybody who had grown up under Nazi rule. She even opened the door wider and stepped back.

The policeman spoke in a polite but authoritative voice. "I wish to speak to *Herr* Mörschel."

"Please come in," the maid said. She took them into the parlor. "I shall inform *Herr* Mörschel of your presence." She curtsied to the two visitors then hurried away to fetch her employer.

Moments later a stocky bald man walked into the room with an expression of confusion on his face. "*Guten tag.* May I help you?"

The policeman stated, "I am here to serve you with eviction papers. You are to move from these premises within the next thirty days."

"*Es ist nicht in Ordnung*! Why must I leave my house?"

Now Arnsteiner spoke up. "This is not *your* house. It is *my* house."

"How can that be?" Mörschel asked. "My family and I have lived here since 1938."

Arnsteiner's eyes flashed pure fury. "And my family lived here since 1893 when my father purchased it. He is —*was*—Doctor Levi Arnsteiner and he raised a family here."

Mörschel's face paled. "*Ich...uh...Ich verstehe nicht!*"

"You understand all right. My parents, two brothers and sister were arrested in this house. They were taken with other Jews in railroad cattle cars to Auschwitz Concentration Camp. They died in the gas chamber and were turned into ashes in the camp crematorium. This residence was stolen from us by Nazi storm troopers!"

The policeman spoke up. "It is a known fact that when Jewish people were taken from their homes, members of the Nazi party were allowed to move in. And there is evidence of your membership in that political organization."

"But I was a minor official!" Mörschel gasped. "I was arrested and investigated and cleared of any war crimes. This was by the American authorities."

"How ironic!" Arnsteiner remarked. "And I am taking back my family home by permission of those same American authorities."

Mörschel hung his head. He was going to be punished for his wartime politics after all. The man was further cowed by Arnsteiner's physical appearance. He was tall and tough looking with broad shoulders.

Arnsteiner looked at the walls. "We had expensive paintings by the old masters hanging in here. Five of them to be exact."

"I swear I know nothing of them!" Mörschel protested. "When I moved in the house there were no paintings anywhere inside. Not even furniture." He made a sweeping gesture across the parlor. "I purchased all that is here."

"I am going to take a look around."

He began a tour of his family residence, going from room to room, examining the walls. Old memories swept over him and he felt the ghostly presence of his departed parents and siblings in each one. Arnsteiner went to his old room and looked out the window. He could see the park below where he used to play as a boy.

———

DAVID ARNSTEINER HAD BEEN BORN IN 1913, THE youngest child of the family. He was a mischievous boy and a wild teenager. He always carried a chip on his shoulder and engaged in numerous fistfights with other boys. Additionally, young David did poorly in school and drove the rabbi mad in Hebrew classes. After being punished for his behavior he would sometimes run away. Young David even had some trouble with the local police. His father Doctor Levi Arnsteiner was about to give up on his son, but when the boy was sixteen in 1929, representatives of a Zionist organization visited their synagogue.

The Zionists were dedicated to establishing an Israeli state in Palestine. The speaker was a charismatic man who not only sought donations to finance their cause, but also asked for volunteers to go to the Holy Land to make preparations for creating a Jewish nation. He spoke of the kibbutz collective farms where young people lived and worked as they laid down the foundations of the new country to come. He spoke of enemies, both Arab and European, who sought to defeat their cause.

"We Jews have faced death and hardships over numerous centuries, but as God's chosen people we shall rise and conquer. In the end, we will bring back our race's homeland."

For the first time in his life, David saw goals and dreams that impressed him as worth fighting for. He appealed to his father to give him permission to go to Palestine and live on a kibbutz. At first his mother was horrified by the idea, but Dr. Arnsteiner decided it would be good for the youngster. It was an excellent chance for David to learn to work hard, adapt to discipline and benefit the struggles of Zionism. All at the same time.

David proved his father right.

He moved into the hard labor environment of the farming community and enthusiastically adapted to the privation and culture. David picked up the Hebrew language quickly, but he kept his opinion of the alphabet and the writing of it from right to left to himself. At any rate, he labored like a peasant in the fields, carried a gun when it was his turn to be on guard duty, and made himself useful in all the aspects and activities of the communal group.

When World War II broke out in Europe, many of the young Jewish men desired to fight the Nazis and enlisted in British Army units that were stationed in Palestine. David at the age of twenty-seven, was one of those who was accepted. He was assigned to a Palestinian Jewish battalion and fought in the Greek Campaign of 1941. One of the advantages of his service, other than killing Nazis, was developing a fluency in the English language.

Then in 1944 President Franklin D. Roosevelt of the United States and Prime Minister Winston Churchill of Great Britain were instrumental in the establishment of a Jewish Brigade.

David, now a captain, went with his comrades to the British Eighth Army and fought in the Italian Campaign.

In 1946 after the Allied victory, the Jewish Brigade was demobilized. He remained in Europe and joined a group of discharged brigade members dedicated to tracking down German war criminals who had committed atrocities against the Jews. David's efficiency and good leadership made him stand out in those activities and eventually he was sought to join a secret organization in righting wrongs done against their people. The group was well-funded from drives conducted in the United States, thus were equipped with almost unlimited resources. They became known as *Tsad'yod-mem*: The Hunters.

David Arnsteiner was given a small Citroën sedan for transportation. When that process was finalized, the first official act David Arnsteiner performed was to take possession of his old family home.

———

BACK IN WICHITA, KANSAS, ON THE MORNING after the date at Western Danceland, Dwayne and Donna Sue sat at the counter in her apartment eating a hearty breakfast of toast, eggs and bacon. They had made awkward love the night before because of being apart for so long as well as being drunk. When they awoke they had sex once again. This time it was enjoyable and most satisfying for each.

Dwayne dabbed ketchup from a bottle on his fried eggs and looked over at her. "I hope like hell we're taking up where we left off." She gazed back with a deep sincere affection.

"I hope like hell we are, too," Donna Sue replied. "I always felt some regret that..." She paused a moment. "Just let me say I'm really crazy about this new Dwayne Wheeler. The way you were before was—"

He interrupted. "Why don't we just forget all that."

"Good idea. More coffee?"

"Yes, please. A half a cup will do."

She went to the stove and brought back the percolator. After serving him she resumed her seat. They ate in contented moments of silence thoroughly enjoying each other's presence. It was true Donna Sue was amazed at the change in him. He was a different person altogether and a few of the traits he maintained from the past were good ones.

She asked, "Are you through with Mister Dawson's case?"

"Yeah," he said. "I can talk about it with you. He was afraid his wife was having an affair with another man. She wasn't."

Donna Sue laughed. "All the stenos knew about it."

"How the hell would they know?"

"Those gals know everything that goes on, Dwayne. They work within every aspect of Dawson Construction's operations. They pick up all sorts of information that leak out among the employees. And that goes for me, too."

"So you women knew all about my caper, huh?"

"And we also knew you wouldn't find a man in Gloria's life."

"Well, Miss Connors, you ladies must be pretty sure of yourselves."

"Gloria Dawson is a lesbian."

Dwayne stopped his fork in mid-air between his food and mouth. "What?"

"She's a lesbian," Donna Sue repeated. "The woman she visits is her lover. That's why she spends weekends with her, telling Mister Dawson she's visiting her family in Hutchinson."

"I'll be damned."

"Would you like some more coffee?"

"Nope. Just pour me out a big tumbler of scotch instead."

Donna Sue gave him a big grin. "If you're ever hired by Mister Dawson again, I'll introduce you to the steno-graphic pool. I'm sure they'll be able to answer any questions you might have."

"I guess I'd have to split my fee with 'em, huh?"

CHAPTER 7

A week after Pete and Sybil Van Dyke departed for New York City, Dwayne received a telephone call from the U.S. Post Office in downtown Wichita. He responded quickly, going to the registered mail window and signing for a thick cardboard tube addressed to him. It was two feet long and three inches in diameter. Although not particularly heavy, there was still a bit of a heftiness to it.

He drove directly to Secure Vault Rentals and checked in for an escort. A clerk led the way from the reception area to the clientele chambers. Dwayne waited until the businesslike man fetched his strongbox. They went through the key routine, then the attendant withdrew.

Dwayne turned the handle, pulled the lid up and placed the tube inside. Now he noted the words **NUMMERNSCHILD I** on the label. He also read the words **LUFTPOST / AIR MAIL** stamped across it. His name and phone number were below that, but not his office or apartment address.

He wasn't sure what *nummernschild* meant, but he

would be going by the number alone when it came to managing the package. He closed the lid and pulled on the handle to make sure the strongbox was closed.

With that duty done, he pressed a button on the wall to summon the clerk. When the man arrived, they used their keys to relock the container.

———

DAVID ARNSTEINER DROPPED IN AT HIS HOUSE to check the progress Fritz Mörschel was making in getting out of the residence. He found the ex-Nazi's attitude had turned from sad acceptance to arrogant stubbornness. "I cannot possibly be out of here by the deadline set for me."

Arnsteiner remained calm. "That's unfortunate, *Herr* Mörschel. Not for me, but for you."

"You are being most unkind to me, *Herr* Arnsteiner."

Fury filled Arnsteiner in a single instant. He struck Mörschel hard enough to knock him to the floor, then kicked the man in the ribcage several times. Next the Jew grabbed the Nazi by the shirt and pulled him to his feet. "Your lot murdered my family, you wretched son of a bitch!" He slapped Mörschel's face. "They suffered fear and humiliation!" He cuffed the man's ears. "You inflicted a horrible agonizing death on them!" He punched the frightened ex-Nazi with a hard straight right to the face.

The man screamed and fell to th' floor, rolling around, weeping in pain.

"And you complain that I am being most *unkind* to you?"

Mörschel stifled his groaning, now fearing for his life.

Arnsteiner walked over to a chair and picked it up. He carried the piece of furniture to the door and flung it out into the street. He grabbed a coffee table and did the same thing. Then a lamp. Then another chair.

"That's all I'm going to do for you. So get up and start working, you miserable worm!"

Mörschel struggled to his feet, sobbing

Arnsteiner delivered three rapid stinging slaps to the man's face. "Now! Are you going to be out of here on the proper date?"

Mörschel groaned out, "*Ja.*"

"You show me some respect, you measly worm!"

"*Jawohl!*" Mörschel bleated in the proper respectful way a German underling is supposed to address a social or military superior.

———

THE OFFICE OF THE HUNTERS WAS LOCATED IN the market area of Sommerfeld. It was a storefront with a large window that had a sign in English lettered across it.

DISPLACED PERSONS REGISTRATION OFFICE

The entrance into the place was a dirty scratched-up door. David Arnsteiner knocked and stepped inside to a small vestibule where a young woman sat at a battered desk. "Hello, David."

"Good afternoon, Pili. I received a message that Yitzhak wants to see me."

"He certainly does," the receptionist replied. "Go right in."

Arnsteiner went through an interior door into a room with desks, filing cabinets, bookshelves and other furniture of a business nature. A number of very busy men and women carefully scanned, wrote and labeled various classes of papers and documents.

He went to the back where a heavily bearded man by the name Yitzhak Cohen sat. Cohen looked up from a file he was examining. "Hello, David. Glad you got here."

"What is so important?"

"You are getting a new assignment," Cohen informed him. "It is a most important situation that I thought perfect for you."

"Good! I hope it is an assassination of some *SS* criminal."

"Oh, it is much more sophisticated than that. I remember a few days ago you mentioned some missing paintings of great value that had been in your parents' home before the war."

Arnsteiner nodded his head. "So?"

"So there have been some leads on artwork that have been called to our attention. The Americans found a great deal of artistic treasures with a special unit they had formed for that purpose. All of it was out of Jewish homes. The stuff had been hidden in manmade caves, warehouses and other locations. They've pretty well covered every place there is. And now, they have scaled down their efforts."

"I am interested," Arnsteiner declared.

"I have been handed a list of missing artwork. It is not complete, but has a good number of paintings on it. They are worth millions of American dollars. We think many of them may have been smuggled out of Europe or soon will be. If we do not take action, they will either disappear or be put into museums and galleries. If this latter possibility occurs, it would take years to retrieve them through legal means."

"Who is behind all this?"

"The best we know is that it is an unknown secret organization of *SS* officers who wish to hide the art, then make sales to build up significant funds in their coffers." He shrugged. "Beyond that we are totally ignorant."

"How am I supposed to get started on this project?"

"You take this list," Cohen said, shoving it across the desk to him. "Match it up against what the Americans have discovered. Any that are not there can be presumed to be in the hands of the Neo-Nazis in new hiding places only they know."

"I shall start with the five paintings missing from my house," Arnsteiner said. "Excuse me for a few minutes."

He walked over to an empty desk where a typewriter was located. He sat down in front of the machine, then began dredging up information from down deep in his memory. When satisfied, he started typing the list of masterpieces that belonged to his family by artists' names and the titles of their works.

- LIPPI / MADONNA AND CHILD
- VELAZQUEZ / CARPENTER OF SEVILLE
- RUBENS / THE WOODSMAN AND WOMEN
- HALS / PEASANT WOMAN WITH CAT
- REMBRANDT / SAMSON AT THE TEMPLE

It was hunt-and-peck typing but he got it down well enough for a reference. He pulled the paper out of the typewriter and walked over to Cohen's desk. "I have managed to remember enough about the titles of my family's art to put them down on paper. Now I need a contact if I am ever to have a chance of tracking them down."

"Ah, yes," Cohen acknowledged. He opened his desk drawer and pulled out a business card. "Here's the gentleman to see. He is an Englishman working in the Bureau of Property Recovery here in the American Sector. His name is Henry Hawkins."

"What is the story on the fellow?"

"He is a retired major from the British Army."

"That is handy," Arnsteiner stated. "We can form a suitable rapport because of my service with the British when I was in the Jewish Brigade."

"Exactly," Cohen agreed. "That is why you were chosen for this assignment. The major has spent quite a bit of time on the search and recovery of items stolen from missing or deceased Jews. The Americans were evidently so impressed with him that they have posted him on their team. He does not have an abundance of authority, but gives advice and goes out on investigations. That will be to our advantage. Henry Hawkins will not mind delving into any paperwork that becomes necessary in this search for works of art."

"I shall contact the man as soon as possible," Arnsteiner stated enthusiastically.

CHAPTER 8

Dwayne picked up a half dozen more tubes of art in the two weeks following the first arrival. He also received a phone call from Pete Van Dyke checking in to see how the routine was going.

"It's a piece of cake," Dwayne reported. "Downright boring actually."

"That's good. But don't let your guard down. Be suspicious and pessimistic while you're performing your tasks."

"Right. I've always got my reliable .45 semi-auto in my shoulder holster."

"Atta boy! I'll be in contact with you later."

After he hung up, Dwayne drove to the Nash automobile dealership on East Kellogg. He'd made an appointment to see about purchasing a 1948 Nash Suburban station wagon. It was a "woody" version of the Ambassador called the Suburban, and cost $2,1oo. He'd first driven one during his undercover assignment for the F.B.I. and admired its reliability and handling. That particular model was owned by an Irish gang out of Boston that he had infiltrated.

Currently Dwayne was earning the $200 a week and he figured each month as 4-1/3 weeks. Thus he would be receiving $867 monthly or an annual income of $10,400. That, when compared to the average annual $3100 for most Americans, now made him upper class.

Dwayne made the car deal putting down half the price and financing the balance. The Suburban had to be prepped for finalization of the sale and he left the dealership, returning to his office. After arriving, he checked in with his answering service and there were no calls. That was fine with him since in the late afternoon he always picked up Donna Sue after work and they went out for supper. Most of the time the routine ended up with him spending the evening at her place. Of course this included a session of lovemaking for the horny couple who had renewed their lust and love for each other.

———

THE NASH DEALERSHIP PHONED DWAYNE AT HIS office in the morning two days after the deal had been made. He was informed the vehicle was prepped and ready, and he could pick up it up anytime. He drove the Buick from his office to his apartment building and parked it, then called for a cab for a ride to pick up the Suburban.

The timing worked out quite well for Dwayne and he was able to drive over to Dawson Construction and meet Donna Sue for a lunch date. When she came out the door she saw him standing by the new car.

"What's this, Dwayne?"

"My dear," he replied rather dramatically, "this trendy

ultra-modern, luxurious vehicle you are looking at is a 1948 Nash Suburban Station Wagon. I have just purchased it. And I might add that my credit record was good enough to have me approved for the deal."

"Oh my God! You weren't kidding when you said you were in the chips."

"I could never fool you, Donna Sue. I think you remember that."

"I certainly do. And you tried to pull the wool over my eyes a lot. Especially when it came to the money you lost playing the ponies." She walked around the Suburban. "I guess you traded in your Buick on it, huh?"

"Nope," he said, reaching in his pocket and pulling out a key ring with two keys on it. "These are for the Buick's ignition and trunk. I'm going to let you have it. Now you won't have to ride the bus anymore. And I can wait in your apartment for you to come home from work."

"Oh, thank you so much, Dwayne. But I can't afford the upkeep."

"It's still my car, sweetie. I'll pay for the insurance and maintenance. And give you a gasoline allowance to boot."

"Dwayne, I can pay for the gas. It's not that expensive."

"Okay. Let's go to lunch and this evening I'll come back here to pick you up and take you over to *my* place and you can drive the Buick back to *your* place."

Donna Sue was overwhelmed by this gesture. In the past when they were lovers the only presents he'd given her had been occasional flowers and boxes of candy. And those were only on her birthday, Christmas and when he'd done something that had really pissed her off.

It was a few minutes before quitting time when Donna Sue saw Dwayne drive up in the station wagon. She was excited about having a car at her disposal. It meant being able to go shopping, run errands and other activities that required her to go out-and-about. As soon as the lobby clock showed five p.m. she grabbed her purse and hurried out to the Nash in the parking lot.

It was a twenty-five-minute trip from the construction company to Dwayne's apartment house due to the rush-hour traffic. Dwayne felt lucky when he arrived at his apartment building and spotted a parking space directly behind the Buick. They quickly exited the Nash and went straight to the older car.

"Get in," he said. "I'll follow you back to your place. I'll park the Nash and you can drive us over to that restaurant you like at Hillside and Central."

Donna Sue positioned herself behind the wheel in the Buick. She turned the ignition key and stepped down on the starter pedal. A pleasurable sensation caused her to smile at the sound of the engine. She glanced back at Dwayne in the rearview mirror, then eased out into the street.

———

Yitzhak Cohen made an appointment for David Arnsteiner to meet with Major Henry Hawkins at the Bureau of Property Recovery in the American Sector. Hawkins was established in a two-story building that had served as the conscription center for the German military during the war. An M.P. directed Arnsteiner to an office at the end of the second floor hall. He ascended the stairs and walked down to the door, knocked and responded to the invitation to enter.

A man appearing to be in his mid-thirties with the longish haircut favored by the British upper-class, greeted Arnsteiner. He had bushy eyebrows and a neatly trimmed moustache that turned up at the ends. He stood up, offering his hand. "You must be Mister Arnsteiner."

"That I am, Major. It is a pleasure to make your acquaintance."

"Well, shall we sit whilst you tell me how I may be of assistance to you?"

Arnsteiner settled down. "By the way, I served in the Jewish Brigade with the British Army. That is where I learned to speak English."

"Splendid chaps the Jewish Brigade! That leads me to think you must have lived in Palestine before the war."

"I was born and raised in Germany, but went there to serve the Zionist cause," Arnsteiner explained. "At any rate, I am now assigned to the same duties you are engaged in. Except I am only interested in recovering property that belonged to Jews. As a matter of fact, I just took back possession of my family home. That gave me the satisfaction of evicting the former Nazi who had been living there."

"Good show!"

"This may seem a bit selfish on my part, but I would like to begin my duties by searching out five paintings that hung in that home. I typed out the painters and the titles of the art."

"Well, I can start you out straight off," Hawkins said. He got up and walked over to a filing cabinet. After fetching a rather large bundle of paper, he returned to his desk and laid the documents down. "All recovered paintings are listed here by artists in alphabetical order."

Arnsteiner pulled his typed list from his coat pocket and began going through the inventory. Since he only had five to check out it didn't take him long. "None of mine are here," he said. "That means I am going to have to go deep into this recovery project."

"I certainly wish you luck."

"By the way," Arnsteiner said. "What regiment did you serve with?"

"Grenadier Guards," Hawkins replied. "I was on the staff as quartermaster. Not exactly a frontline billet, but I suppose I did my bit."

"I am sure you did, Major. Well, good day and thank you for your assistance."

Hawkins watched Arnsteiner leave. "That's one bloody Hebrew I shall have to keep my eyes on," he muttered to himself.

CHAPTER 9

David Arnsteiner did additional investigating the day after his visit to Major Henry Hawkins. He went to the headquarters in both the French and British sectors to check into additional property recoveries. He found he needn't have bothered since they had turned all their information over to the Americans and it obviously was funneled into Major Henry Hawkins' small office.

Arnsteiner took time for a quick lunch in a *kaffehaus* in the British Sector then went directly to visit Yitzhak Cohen in the headquarters of the *Tsad'yod-mem* A.K.A. the Displaced Persons Registration Office. After being admitted into the man's presence, Arnsteiner sat down and gave him a hard look across the desk. "What do you know about Major Henry Hawkins?"

"I have already informed you all that I know about the gentleman."

"Tell me, Yitzhak. Did you make any inquiries about him through your sources of intelligence?"

Now Cohen was worried. "Do you have a problem, David?

"Well...let me see. When I inquired about his war service before his retirement, he told me he was the quartermaster in the Grenadier Guards. That regiment is part of the elite and exclusive Brigade of Guards. The officers of that unit are a snobbish bunch. They all attended public schools in Great Britain that, as we know, are not public at all. Those institutions of learning are for the upper class British. Therefore, they consider themselves much better than anyone else in military or civilian environs."

Cohen shrugged. "So? Everybody is aware how snobbish and clannish they are."

Arnsteiner nodded his agreement. "They are so elitist that the gentlemen officers think it is beneath them to serve as quartermasters since it smacks of being a shopkeeper. That is the section of the staff that deals with supply. Thus, a quartermaster sergeant is always commissioned and assigned to the quartermaster slot when there is a vacancy. This is a meticulously observed custom in the Brigade of Guards."

Cohen repeated, "So?"

"So our Major Henry Hawkins is an upper class British gentleman, undoubtedly a member of the gentry and therefore would not—I say again—*would not* accept an assignment as a quartermaster."

"Perhaps as a former enlisted man he was putting on airs."

"British officers were our commanders in the Jewish Brigade," Arnsteiner explained. "And I can guarantee it would be impossible for some enlisted Cockney or other working class Englishman to imitate the way the upper class speaks."

Cohen reached for his phone. "I know an intelligence officer stationed in the upper echelons of the American high command. That is Lieutenant Colonel Roger Kobelski who is a fine Jewish gentleman."

"Excellent," Arnsteiner stated. "Let's see if that fine Jewish gentleman can find out about Major Hawkins."

———

DONNA SUE, LIKE DWAYNE, EXPERIENCED emotional issues after their romantic and sexual relationship re-emerged. Her initial breakup with him was not sudden. It evolved over several months when she made a personal vow to herself that she would go far beyond her work as a waitress. At that time Donna Sue was employed in the Jayhawker Restaurant, an eatery that was much more a diner than a restaurant since it had no booths. The customers sat on stools along a counter that ran the length of the small narrow building. It was located on West Douglas Avenue across the street from the OK Barbershop.

Dwayne Wheeler frequented that tonsorial business for several reasons. It was where his late father worked as a barber, several bookies operated their businesses in the back of the place, and there were showers he could use. This latter feature was important to him because the boarding house where he lived had a single bathroom and a tub for bathing. The shamus wasn't the least bit persnickety, but even he recognized the poor sanitation of sharing the facilities with eight other guys.

Dwayne also ate regularly at the Jayhawker Restaurant. At that time Donna Sue was bothered by several issues in her life that made her somber and unhappy. It's not surprising that at that time she had no desire for a permanent relationship with a man. But that feeling dissipated a great deal after she met Dwayne Wheeler. He actually never tried to pick her up when he came into the restaurant, but she thought he was cute with his boyish handsomeness and charm, and wouldn't have minded if he asked her out. But he never did.

Then they ran into each other one Saturday night at the country-western nightclub Western Danceland when she was with a girlfriend. Dwayne asked Donna Sue for a dance. She acquiesced and the evening evolved into a date-like situation. Another guy eventually picked up the girl-friend and away they went. That left Donna Sue in the lurch, so Dwayne ended up giving her a ride home. They made a date for a return to the rustic nightclub the next weekend. After that, going out together became a habit, then rapidly involved into the couple becoming an item.

Dwayne was broke a lot of times, and Donna Sue always furnished him meals in the Jayhawker when he was short on cash. She also provided him with morale boosts when he was locked out of his office for getting behind in the rent. That meant he also had to sneak in and out of the boardinghouse where he lived. Those unhappy finan-cial conditions were the result of the crazy long shot bets he made with the bookies across the street in the barbershop.

Donna Sue's feelings of affection for Dwayne grew, but sometimes she felt it was similar to a fondness for a younger, somewhat irresponsible and immature brother.

Donna Sue, like Dwayne, had a rough life as a child after her father had run off with another woman. That left her mother and the four kids in desperate circum-stances. Donna Sue was the oldest which meant she had to quit school to help her mother at her job of cleaning offices in downtown Wichita. The pay was miserably low, forcing them to spend Saturdays doing long hours of laundry and ironing for several well-to-do ladies. It was hard work filling their old washing machine with water; putting in the Rinso soap flakes and the clothes. When that part was finished, the machine had to be drained for the next load. Meanwhile they had to soak the clean duds twice in rinse tubs before running them through the wringer. Then the clothing had to be taken out and hung on the line strung between the house and alley fence to dry. The next step was ironing.

On Sundays they took the finished laundry to their customers. This required riding the bus with at least three transfers. It was exhausting and depressing, but between that and the cleaning job, they earned an average of fifteen dollars a week. Mrs. Connors and Donna Sue managed to keep everyone fed and a roof over their heads.

Donna Sue had begun working at the Jayhawker Restaurant before the war when she was just eighteen and lately divorced after two years of marriage. Her husband was a truck driver ten years older than she. He had a bad habit of coming home drunk and raping her, smothering any notions that she had been carried away to some castle-in-the-sky by a prince charming. After a couple of years, the lout simply disappeared and was never heard of again. The divorce was a mere matter of paperwork.

She hated waitressing, but relief came from that line of work on December 7, 1941. The Japanese made a sneak attack on the American naval base at Pearl Harbor, Hawaii. This launched the United States into World War II and began a gigantic industry of manufacturing guns, munitions, airplanes and other matériel needed for the conflict. The Boeing Aircraft Company published a want ad for workers in their Wichita factory, and with the war time draft on, the manufacturer was hiring women as well as men.

Donna Sue wasted no time in calling it quits to

slinging hash and applied for a position. She was accepted and joined the ranks of those working females who became collectively known as "Rosie the Riveter."

Donna Sue was a fast learner and impressed her supervisor enough for him to choose her to attend the company training program as a welder. When the short but effective apprenticeship ended, she was assigned to the B-17 bombers with a rating as a Class A welder. With that promotion she began making a hefty ninety cents an hour with plenty of overtime. Eventually she became a quality control inspector of the other welders. This was quite an accomplishment for a woman, and an article was written about her in the company newsletter complete with a photo. Donna Sue saved a copy of the publication but rarely looked at it in later years because of the anger and frustration it stimulated.

Donna Sue met her second husband at Boeing. They worked different shifts, seeing each other mostly on Sundays. The arrangement worked out well for their relationship, but one day a production delay resulted in her coming home early. She found her hubby in bed with a neighbor woman. He and his paramour fled her wrath, and a divorce followed within a year.

When the war ended, Donna Sue was let go like all the other women at the plant. With jobs cut, only the men were kept on. It wiped out all her hard work and accomplishments in an instant. She went back to the Jayhawker Restaurant, and was not happy about the unfairness of the situation. With very little education and no hopes for better employment, she developed a rather jaded outlook on the world.

And, as the old saying goes, there was nothing more she could do but grin and bear it; without many grins.

———

AFTER THE STINGING EMBARRASSMENT OF BEING fired from a make-work job for not agreeing to be Brian Murchison's courtesan, Donna Sue settled for the receptionist position at Dawson Construction. She endured an instant whirlwind of nostalgia and regret when Dwayne Wheeler showed up in the company lobby. But his casual invitation to take her to dinner at the Stockyards Restaurant eased her anxiety.

Donna Sue Connors had always loved Dwayne Wheeler, but he failed to fill her need for a supportive partner. Even though he had solved two well-known murder cases in Wichita, his basic attitude was made up of carelessness, recklessness, unpredictability and other irritating qualities that made her expect the worst from him. That was the main motive for going to business college to learn secretarial skills. She could leave the Jayhawker Restaurant and not be dependent on any man for her wellbeing.

When Murchison hired her, they began dating and Donna Sue eventually went to bed with him. It wasn't passion that drove her to having sex, instead it was a symbolic gesture of declaring a final separation from Dwayne.

But now, this new Dwayne Wheeler proved to be a wonderful and unexpected surprise. He required nothing from her and even furnished her with a car. Instead of a boardinghouse, he had a decent apartment, drove a luxury station wagon and was earning a lot of money in his detective work.

CHAPTER 10

A couple of days following David Arnsteiner's visit to Yitzhak Cohen's office, the latter's desk phone rang. "Hello, Yitzhak," a voice said. "This is Roger." Lieutenant Colonel Roger Kobelski was the Jewish gentleman Cohen had called to check out the British officer in the Bureau of Property Recovery. "I have that information on Major Henry Hawkins you asked for."

"Excellent! Fire away."

"Henry Hawkins was in the Grenadier Guards Regiment of the British Army."

"Uh huh," Cohen said.

"He was the regimental quartermaster sergeant."

"Uh huh."

"When the regimental quartermaster was given a medical release from the Army, Henry Hawkins was commissioned a major and took over the post."

"Uh huh."

"And Major Henry Hawkins retired two years ago."

"Uh huh."

"And he died from a heart attack after only a year of retirement," Kobelski continued.

"*Uh oh!*"

Kobelski was confused. "Is there any problem, Yitzhak?"

Cohen nervously cleared his throat before speaking. "Thank you for the information, Roger. I shall get back to you."

———

AFTER THE DATE AT WESTERN DANCELAND, Dwayne and Donna Sue decided they would never return to the redneck establishment. Both agreed the Roadhouse nightclub was much more pleasing for evenings of dining and dancing. Loud arguments, let alone brawls, were not tolerated in its more sophisticated environment.

Since the renewal of their romance, the couple spent all their weekends at Dwayne's apartment. This new procedure began each Friday with him waiting for her to come home from work. As soon as she arrived, the lady gathered up the clothing, cosmetics and other items she would need for the weekend. After that they headed for the Homestyle Restaurant at Central and Hillside for a quick meal. This was followed by a drive to Dwayne's place to prepare for their evening's activities. The first item on this agenda was to make love, then Dwayne allowed Donna Sue to plan out the rest of the weekend's activities.

There was a one-time break in this established tradition. Just for the hell of it, instead of the usual eating place, they went downtown to the Jayhawker Restaurant where Donna Sue had once slung hash. Neither had been there since their breakup, and they didn't recognize either of the two waitresses when they walked in. But just as they sat down on a couple of stools, there was a loud shout through the kitchen's serving window.

"Donna Sue! Dwayne!"

Arnie Dawkins the cook came out to the counter. "It can't be you!"

"It's us, all right," Dwayne said. He and Donna Sue both noticed he looked pretty much the same but had obviously aged a bit.

"Where is Maisie?" Donna Sue asked.

"She ain't here no more," Arnie said. "When her husband came back from Korea they was transferred to Nellis Air Force Base in Nevada." He rubbed his hands together. "Okay, Dwayne! I know what you want. A grilled cheese sandwich and French fries." He snapped his fingers at the taller waitress. "Get my buddy here an Orange Crush outta the cooler, okay?" He looked at Donna Sue. "Whatta you want?"

"I remember your egg salad sandwiches," Donna Sue replied. "I'll have one of those and potato chips."

"You got 'em, honey," Arnie said, going back into the kitchen.

The tall waitress set a bottle of Orange Crush in front of Dwayne. "I see you two are old friends of Arnie's, huh?"

"You bet," Dwayne said.

The shorter waitress walked up. "Arnie talks about you guys a lot." She smiled at Dwayne. "He said you was a real good detective."

"Yeah!" the taller waitress remarked. "Arnie said you was just like them guys on the radio and in the movies."

The shorter waitress turned toward Donna Sue

saying, "Arnie said you went to secretary school and got a good job."

"That I did."

The shorter waitress sighed. "I wish I could become a secretary but I didn't finish high school."

Donna Sue started to tell her how she studied a GED course for a diploma to become a secretary. But she decided it might sound boastful if the girl had no decent schooling. Donna Sue had personal memories of that embarrassment in her early life.

As usual not many customers were in the place since it was early evening. The Jayhawker's busiest hours were during the day, especially at lunch. A lot of people who had jobs in the downtown area came in at that time. Sometimes a few had to stand and wait for a stool to be vacated before they could be served.

Arnie came out of the kitchen and placed their orders on the counter. "I seen Dwayne go into the barbershop across the street now and again. I was always disappointed when he didn't come over here."

The statement brought back the hurt feelings Dwayne endured after the breakup with Donna Sue. He couldn't bear going into the eatery because of the memories it stirred up. He took a swallow of Orange Crush. "I didn't have to take showers there no more. And I've stopped betting on the ponies as much as I used to."

"Well, anyhow it's good to see you," Arnie said. "You guys come in now and then, okay?"

"We'll do that," Donna Sue said. She, too, had feelings of nostalgia about the restaurant. At those times, even when she and Brian Murchison were lovers, she missed the shamus and his antics that were both boyish and risky.

After finishing their meals, Dwayne and Donna Sue

ordered slabs of pie and coffee. Suddenly Donna Sue remembered Arthur Manger the owner. "How's Art been?"

"He died, Donna Sue," Arnie said. "About a year back. His wife Agatha still runs the place. She shows up to get the receipts a couple of times a week."

Another ten minutes passed and the pies were eaten and the coffee drunk. Dwayne and Donna Sue made their goodbyes and took final looks around the restaurant before walking out.

Both knew they would never go back to the Jayhawker again.

———

IT WAS NINE O'CLOCK WHEN DWAYNE AND Donna Sue showed up at the Roadhouse nightclub to renew their duo patronage. The two greeter-bouncers at the entrance, Jack Wallace and Denny Tarball, gave the couple wide grins.

"We knew you was coming!" Jack happily exclaimed.

"Yeah!" Denny said. "We always look at the reservation list to see if any important folks would be showing up."

"And there your names was," Jack said.

Denny interjected, "And I said to Jack, I said, looky there! Some *real* important folks are gonna show up tonight! Dwayne and Donna Sue! Together!"

Dwayne joined in the enthusiasm. "Yep! We're together again. And gonna stay that way."

"Well, you two nice people enjoy yourselves," Jack said.

The couple went inside and approached the maître d'. He had been hired after Kansas became a wet state so didn't know them well, although he recognized Donna Sue as being in the club with Brian Murchison several times. As a professional, he knew enough not to inquire as to the rich man's absence. He merely took their names, then snapped his fingers. Teresa Jansen, a waitress, appeared.

Like Jack and Denny, Teresa didn't hide her surprise. Her mouth dropped open, then she asked. "Are you guys an item again? I'm glad to see—"

The maître d' interrupted. "Please escort the lady and gentleman to their table!"

After being seated, they were approached by Elmer Pettibone, the owner of the club. "I couldn't believe my eyes when I saw you two on the reservation list."

"Yep," Dwayne said. "We turned it all back on again."

Pettibone had been one of Wichita's leading bootleggers during Kansas' dry years. Dwayne often drove down to a place near Terral, Oklahoma to pick up illegal liquor for him.

"Well, enjoy yourselves this evening," Pettibone urged them. "Your drinks are gonna be on the house."

"Hey! Thanks, Elmer," Dwayne replied.

Thus began an evening that was destined to reoccur many times. The couple imbibed cocktails, danced and thoroughly enjoyed each other's company. Donna Sue was particularly happy. After an upsetting and embarrassing situation, she had now drifted into an incredibly good life with Dwayne as her lover. He was attentive, generous, and responsible. There were times when she experienced a rush of giddiness that made her feel like a teenager.

———

THEY LEFT THE ROADHOUSE AT TWO A.M.
Instead of driving to the apartment house, Dwayne drove
into a parking garage a block away. He had rented a space
in the building where a night watchman was on duty. The
Nash station wagon was an expensive car and he decided it
wasn't a good idea to leave it parked outside overnight.

CHAPTER 11

Major Henry Hawkins reached across his desk and picked up the papers that an administrative assistant had just dropped into his inbox. He lit a cigarette and after a couple of languid draws turned his attention to the documents.

Like most bureaucracies, the Bureau of Property Recovery kept itself mired in unnecessary paperwork. This was done by the bureau's leadership to give the impression to their superiors that they were extremely busy while successfully accomplishing their goals. However, those unnecessary workloads were largely ignored by the harried staff. Thus Hawkins didn't expect much as he thumbed through the contents looking for something that interested him.

After tossing out the least desirable items, the major turned to the one he considered important. It was the latest list of discovered property that had been stolen by the Nazis. Unfortunately, the breakup of relations between the Western Allies and the Soviet Union had gone from bad to worse. Under those circumstances the hunt for treasure was sabotaged by the Russians. If they found anything of value, they kept it for themselves to send back to Moscow. That included factory machinery and all kinds of trucks.

Under those circumstances, the frustrated Allies could only deal with property hidden in concealed places throughout their sectors of West Germany.

Hawkins quickly scanned the contents with labels reading **CLOCKS, CLOTHING, FURNITURE, JEWELRY**, until he reached **PAINTINGS**. He pulled that section out and put it in a large envelope, then rang the bell on his desk. *Frau* Schweitzer his secretary appeared in the office door.

"Yes, Major?" she inquired.

"Please contact Bruno in the mailroom and have him come up here. Tell him it's for a delivery."

Frau Schweitzer quickly obeyed and Bruno Schlagger appeared within three minutes. He was a large, muscular man in his late thirties. He walked up to Hawkins' desk and came to a halt, standing in the position of attention. *"Jawohl, Herr Major!"*

"You've just done it again, Bruno! I've told you a hundred times not to carry on as a soldier. Our circumstances make it very unwise to do so."

"I am sorry, Major."

Hawkins held out the envelope. "Take this to *Herr* Von Leipinger. Tell him they just arrived in my office this morning."

"Right away, Major."

"Now, however, remember to salute *him* when you hand it over," Hawkins said. "That is because you will be at the *Wolflager*. Military discipline is the order of the day there."

"Ja, Major Hawkins," Schlagger said, then made an

immediate exit. He was happy to get out of the confines of the mail room for a drive to the Munich area.

Hawkins leaned back in his chair and lit another cigarette. He was a contented and satisfied man. His life and work were running smoothly without complications. The only unpleasant thing about his present existence was that he had been obligated to temporarily leave his luxury apartment and mistress Lale in Munich. But it was a necessary inconvenience if the conspiracy he was involved in were to succeed.

There in the city of Sommerfeld Hawkins lived with his secretary Griselde Schweitzer in a cheap hotel not far from where they worked. The couple occupied the rooms at the very top of the building. These were more comfortable than the smaller living spaces on the first and second floors. It boasted its own bathroom with an alcove off to the side that served as a small kitchen and dining area.

When he interviewed *Frau* Schweitzer to be his secretary, she presented him with excellent letters of reference from previous employers. He hired the woman because of these impeccable recommendations. But he made it plain that he would expect her to live with him and provide him with sexual favors. She was not offended by the demand since such arrangements were common in the defeated nation.

Most of the population was poverty stricken, lacking tolerable living conditions. *Frau* Schweitzer was desperate for the job and she quickly agreed to his terms. There were other less fortunate women who were forced to sell themselves on the streets for cigarettes and soap. Another extremely good reason to accept the position was that the pay was double what she could make in a conventional German job.

Hawkins had been with unhappy females before and

they did not make satisfactory sexual partners. He lived by the adage that a contented woman was a grateful woman. And, to add some sweetness to his arrangement with *Frau* Schweitzer, Hawkins granted her weekends off so she could visit with her mother and daughter.

The woman was rather plain but did her best to satisfy him sexually. He had to admit she really wasn't so bad a substitute for Lale and at times seemed to enjoy their couplings. *Frau* Schweitzer was a war widow whose husband had been drafted into the German Army and sent to the Eastern Front. He, like many others in the overwhelming defeat in the Battle of Stalingrad in 1943, was listed as missing in action. There was a slim chance he might be a prisoner but the Soviet Union didn't bother to inform the Germans of the identity of POWs. *Frau* Schweitzer's husband could either be living behind barbed wire or buried in an unmarked grave among the rubble of a battlefield.

———

DWAYNE WHEELER WAS NOW WELL SET INTO HIS assignment of receiving tubes of paintings. So far Pete Van Dyke had not given him any instructions to mail the artwork elsewhere. He wondered why the numerous shipments were held up in Wichita, but assumed it was because of some necessary protocol.

Dwayne's work week was simple and convenient. He stayed in his office from eight a.m. to four p.m., waiting for calls from the main U.S. Post Office to inform him about registered deliveries. In the late afternoon when there would be no more mail deliveries, he drove over to Donna Sue's apartment to wait for her to come home from her job. This was the continuance of the pleasant routine they both enjoyed.

The idle hours of his work arrangements gave him time to relax and contemplate this pleasing existence. Generally, when he remembered something or got an idea, the subject leaped into his mind in an unbidden appearance. But now, in this new arrangement, Dwayne had two things he could slowly and deliberately consider.

One was a desire to expand his business so it really matched the new title he had assumed as the Wheeler Detective Agency. For this reason, he decided to be extremely frugal with his enormous salary. He had yet to figure out the exact amount of investment it would take to hire one or two fulltime operatives. He knew several retired cops from the Wichita Police Department who would fit that particular bill. But it would only pay off if they were kept busy.

There were other money-making possibilities such as setting up a private security service. These employees could also direct parking at public events, keep an eye on things at municipal gatherings or deal with shoplifters in local stores. Of course there would be the expense of uniforms. That was also a good market in which banks could use guards as well as drivers to operate their armored truck pickups and deliveries.

Now that he was in that serious mood, the second subject that eased its way into his thoughts was marriage. He was in love with Donna Sue and it was pleasantly obvious that she returned his ardor. The money seemed like a pretty solid base to build on and he was certainly pulling in big dough. That would come in handy for buying a nice house. Because of his discharge for convenience of the government, he couldn't get a G.I. loan like other veterans.

Dwayne, with his feet propped up on his desk, yawned and stretched, then the phone rang. It was the post office with another mailing for him to pick up. He grinned to himself and walked over to get his hat from the rack in the corner of the office. He went to the door and stepped out into the hall, saying to himself, "Hey, Self, I think me and Donna Sue are gonna be taking a long ride on the gravy train."

CHAPTER 12

The early afternoon sun shined through the window onto Major Henry Hawkins' desk. He was back from enjoying a heavy lunch at the restaurant down the street, and was irritated. His displeasure was not because of the quality of the food at the little eatery, but for the fact that he craved a nap after stuffing himself. There was no way the major could doze off at work and get away with it. Too many people walked past his doorway and would notice if he laid his head down to doze. As a man used to afternoon naps, he was extremely unhappy with the situation.

He picked up a recent office memo from his inbox and pretended to peruse it. His eyes kept closing and he shook his head several times to keep from drifting off into slumber. The sudden ringing of the telephone startled him. He lifted the handset and responded, "Hello."

"*Ich suche meine Freunde.*" That translated into English as "I am looking for my friends." Then the line immediately went dead.

Hawkins hung up, now wide awake. He pulled some

papers from his desk drawers and put them in a briefcase. After donning his hat, he walked over to *Frau* Schweitzer's work station. She looked up, surprised at his sudden appearance. "May I help you, Major?"

"I have been summoned to an appointment. I'm not sure when I will return, so you're free to take the rest of the day off and go early to visit your mother and daughter if it pleases you."

"Thank you so much, Major Hawkins!"

He went downstairs to the mailroom and signaled to Bruno Schlagger to come to the entrance. "I've been called to a meeting. Get the car. I'm already late."

The last statement had a special meaning to it and Schlagger knew a serious situation was in the making. He maintained a calm attitude for the benefit of the other clerks. "*Ja freilich, Herr Major.* I will meet you in front of the building."

Schlagger hurried to the Bureau's car park and got into the Volkswagen that had been allocated to the major. He drove around and pulled up to the curb. Nigel Hawthorne quickly got in and Schlagger drove down the street.

———

MANFRED VON LEIPINGER HAD SERVED IN Germany's *Waffen-SS* armored forces during the war. When the fighting ended, the forty-something man had held the rank of *SS-standartenführer* which was the equivalent of a colonel. Von Leipinger was the scion of the old Prussian aristocratic families in which generations of men served in the armies of various *Kaisers*. His entire war service had been on the merciless hell of the Eastern Front.

After the first summer victories scored in the invasion

of the Soviet Union, things went bad in the winter weather. The cold seemed ten times worse than in Germany and the soldiers were poorly equipped to deal with the misery. Their leader Adolf Hitler had expected the Russians to be overpowered before autumn.

Toward the end of the conflict, Von Leipinger commanded a tank regiment that fought desperate delaying actions against the Russians as the German forces retreated. They were finally pushed back to Berlin. That was when Von Leipinger was given explicit and bizarre orders by his corps commander *SS-Gruppenführer* Franz Taubert. The *standartenführer* was to immediately remove himself and his regiment from the city and go west. Once there, he was to surrender his command to the first American forces he found.

Von Leipinger was baffled. This was positive evidence that the war was lost. After surrendering he was to do whatever the Americans demanded. Further orders would be given him sometime in the future by high-ranking *SS* officers after the cessation of hostilities.

———

BRUNO SCHLAGGER KNEW EXACTLY WHERE TO take Nigel Hawthorne. It was an isolated farm in the countryside west of Munich in the German state of Bavaria. After leaving the main highway, the roadways grew rougher the farther they went until the route had diminished to a narrow trail that cut through thick woods. In spite of this, Schlagger had no trouble in driving the small Volkswagen along the rustic track.

They finally descended into a rather low area that was surrounded by an even denser forest. They reached a gate on which a wooden sign was mounted that read:

GENSEND LAZARETT

This translated into English as a military convalescent hospital. Schlagger stopped and an armed guard stepped out from the gatehouse. He was a short, tough-looking Individual with an MP40 submachine gun slung across his chest. The man looked inside the car.

"Hello, Schlagger!" he said, giving an enthusiastic greeting to an old comrade.

"How are you, Horst?" Schlagger replied. The two had endured the freezing and fiery double hells of the Eastern Front together. Schlagger had been the driver of Von Leipinger's tank and Horst Vetter the gunner.

Vetter leaned over and noticed Nigel Hawthorne. "We have been expecting you, Major."

"Does this visit involve anything especially serious?" Hawthorne asked in German. The coded phone call he had received was extremely worrisome.

Vetter shrugged. "I have no idea. *Standartenführer* Von Leipinger will explain it all to you."

Schlagger put the car in gear and continued through the gate until reaching a small meadow. The open area was bare but a stone house was located off to the side under a grove of spruce trees. Hawthorne's military training indicated to him it was a good defensive position with fields of fire over the meadow. Additionally, other firing emplacements could be established in the surrounding forest.

When Schlagger brought the car to a stop in front of the house, a man appeared who hurried around the car to open the door for Hawthorne. He nodded respectfully, saying, "The *standartenführer* is waiting for you. *Bitte folgen Sie mir.*"

Hawthorne did as the man requested and followed him up to the front door and into the house. They went inside and down a hall to a large portal. A man standing there was obviously a guard in spite of civilian attire. He stepped back from the entrance to allow the Englishman to pass.

A person would expect he was entering a medical ward, but it was a large office area with numerous desks. Hawthorne walked down to the end and knocked on the door, stepping inside.

Von Leipinger was obviously relieved to see him. "You do not realize it, Nigel, but you have just had a close call."

Hawthorne nodded. "I was aware of that when I answered the phone. What is going on?"

"Your cover has been compromised. Evidently American military intelligence learned that the real Major Hawkins is dead."

That bothered Hawthorne. "So someone grew suspicious of my cover story. Did our informant know how?"

Von Leipinger shrugged. "The only thing we know is that it came from one of the Jewish agencies. Those clever *Juden* are organized into so many levels, cells and organizations that even they do not know what is going on within their own operations."

"Damn! How is this going to affect us?"

"Not to worry," Von Leipinger assured him. "We have backups and contingencies for every imaginable situation." He grinned. "And you can remove your disguise now."

Hawthorne walked over to a mirror and pulled off the heavy eyebrows that had been placed over his own. He also removed the fake moustache he'd worn for several long weeks. He inspected his reflection, then turned and said, "I believe you have a barber here, correct?"

"Yes," the German said. "Go and get your hair cut and combed back to the way you used to wear it."

"I certainly shall. By the way is your telephone cleared for overseas?"

"Yes. It is secure."

"Excellent!" Hawthorne said. "I'll be able to put in a call to Peter Van Dyke in New York City."

CHAPTER 13

Dwayne and Donna Sue were in the early stages of their Friday evening routine. She had left work and drove the Buick directly to her apartment where he waited for her. There was the usual swap of kisses then she showered and changed while Dwayne leafed idly through a copy of the *Ladies Home Journal*.

After bathing and dressing, Donna Sue packed a bag for the weekend and took some clothes on hangers from her closet. From there they went down to his station wagon for the drive over to the Homestyle Restaurant for an early supper.

Everything was pretty normal during the meal, but Donna Sue sensed a restlessness in Dwayne as she gazed at him across the booth. He seemed on edge, but not in a bad way. He showed an enthusiastic urgency as if there was something important he had to attend to. It didn't take him long to consume all the French fries on his plate, and reach a point where he had only a couple of bites left of his grilled cheese sandwich.

Donna Sue wasn't half way through her meal when

she stopped eating and looked at him. "What's the hurry?"

"What hurry?"

"You're gobbling down that food like eating is an Olympic event!"

He ignored her annoyance. "Whataya say that we don't go to a movie tonight?"

"Why not? We always go to a movie on Friday night."

"We don't have to go *every* Friday night, do we?" Dwayne asked.

"No, I guess not. But tonight the Miller is showing *Notorious* with Cary Grant and Ingrid Bergman."

"We'll go tomorrow night, okay? There's some important stuff I need to talk to you about."

"What sort of important stuff?" Donna Sue asked.

"I can't talk about it now," Dwayne stated. "It's kind of complicated."

"Can't it wait until after the movie?"

"No," he replied. "I even had to make some careful notes so's I wouldn't forget nothing."

"Forget *any*thing," she corrected. "If you didn't forget *nothing* you'd remember *every*thing. Double negatives are—"

"All right. I don't want to forget *anything*."

Donna Sue fell back into silence and stabbed an unoffending piece of roasted squash with her fork. She sensed this was going to be a special Friday evening and she was more than a little apprehensive about it. Dwayne generally approached both good and bad circumstances in the same way. That's why it was so difficult for her to guess what he might have on his mind.

———

SINCE THEY WEREN'T GOING OUT THAT EVENING, Dwayne drove the car into the parking rental garage for the night. He carried Donna Sue's overnight bag from there to the apartment house. The moment they entered Dwayne's digs, she could tell the place was arranged for a critical *tête-à-tête*. There were two coasters side-by-side on the coffee table in front of the sofa. A wine glass was on one of them and a tumbler on the other. A notebook with some scribbling on the opening page was off to one side.

Dwayne went to the refrigerator and grabbed a bottle of chardonnay, then reached up on a shelf for a quart of Jack Daniels Sour Mash Whiskey. Donna Sue watched him. "It appears you really do have something serious to discuss," she remarked as he uncorked the wine.

He walked over and filled her glass. "Don't sit down yet. There's something I want to show you," he said, pouring liquor into his tumbler.

Dwayne led her into the bedroom and over to the closet. He knelt down and pulled out a section of the door jamb and retrieved a roll of bills. "Four thousand dollars," he indicated, then replaced it. "Let's go back to the sofa."

Donna Sue showed a worried frown. "My God! Did you rob a bank?"

"Nope," he replied. "I've been a busy boy during our time apart." They went back to the living room and sat down. He picked up the notebook. "These are my ideas written down."

Donna Sue experienced a strong sensation of concern as she took a sip of wine.

"Okay," he began after a swallow of the Jack Daniels. "I guess you noticed that I changed the name of my business to the Wheeler Detective Agency."

"Yes. And I thought that was better than 'Private

Investigator. Confidential Service.' I believe I told you that."

"Well, now I intend to really have an agency," Dwayne continued. "I want to have several operatives and a secretary to answer the phone and take dictation and type and all that office stuff."

"Are you going to hire me for the job?"

"No."

"Why not?"

"You'll understand after I finish." he answered. "I also want to add a security service of private guards. I'll get contracts from banks, hotels, department stores and other businesses that need protection. The guards will have uniforms except when they need to be nonconspicuous. That'll be—"

"*In*conspicuous," she interrupted. Dwayne had asked her to correct any grammatical errors in his speech. She was confused at first about something that never concerned him before. Now she knew he wanted to make a better impression on potential customers.

"All right. They'll not be wearing uniforms if they got to be *in*-conspicuous for dealing with shoplifters or keeping an eye on things without attracting attention. I'm also thinking of having some cars for private patrols of neighborhoods, construction sites, and places like that."

Now Donna Sue was favorably impressed and any misgivings she had evaporated. This was another indication of the new Dwayne Wheeler. "I think you've got some wonderful ideas!"

He turned to his tablet and began to read off the financial side of the business he planned. He also covered working for the district attorney, bailsmen and other law enforcement agencies. He checked off each item on the list as he first read it aloud then expounded the details.

Three glasses of wine and four of whiskey later between them, he laid the tablet down. "That's it. How's it sound to you?"

"It sounds great, Dwayne. You've really come a long way since we...well...since we drifted apart."

"Yeah. I guess even I can adapt and readapt."

She gave him a fond look. "I can remember when you'd show up at the Jayhawker and just order a cup of coffee. I knew you were short of money and didn't have enough to buy a meal."

"Yeah. And each time you bought me one."

She laughed. "You always went through a routine of turning down my offer. Do you remember what you used to say?"

"Yeah. I'd tell you I wasn't hungry because I ate the day before."

"And I recall the times when you were locked out of your office for not having the rent. You went across the street to the OK Barbershop and used their phone to conduct your business." She wasn't finished. "And I can't even guess how many times you snuck out of Mrs. Busch's rooming house when you owed her money."

"Them were the good ol' days, huh?"

"Not really," Donna Sue stated. "You always made long shot bets with the bookies at the barbershop every time you went over there."

"Yeah. That really pissed you off, didn't it?"

"It sure did. But when you showed up at the Dawson Construction lobby that first time I sensed a big change in you. It was the way you looked and acted that clued me in you were a different man. Then the station wagon and your apartment and giving me the Buick and—"

"Enough of that," Dwayne begged.

"Sure. So when are you going to start this big plan of yours?"

"As soon as I raise enough cash," he answered. "I'm making that 200 bucks a week. I figure if I put away seventy-five bucks of it, I'll have some pretty impressive leverage when I talk with a bank loan officer."

"Then you ought to put that closet money in a bank, too," Donna Sue advised him.

Dwayne winced. "There's a problem. I ain't paid any income tax on that dough so's I'll have to feed it into any accounts a little at a time."

"How did you earn it? And watch the use of *'ain't'*."

"It had to do with a project involving military scrip in Germany," Dwayne replied. "I think you'd be better off if you didn't know all the details. But I'll be paying the taxes on the two hunnerd a week. I'm listing it as capers so I can put that in the bank without arousing suspicion from the I.R.S. I can include that money in the closet a little at a time and not attract any special attention."

"Right," Donna Sue acknowledged. "And it will show the bankers that you're a businessman who makes a profit." She paused and spoke hesitantly. "Is that 200 dollars from a reputable source?"

"Yeah," Dwayne said. "It involves wealthy art collectors who deal secretly between themselves."

"*Among* themselves," Donna Sue corrected once again. This would be the last time she would point out any errors in speech that evening. She knew there was a limit to such agreements.

"Okay," he said with a grin. "Anyhow, that's all I can say about it. It's an undercover thing they use to keep their collections secret *among* themselves. And they know how to handle the project on their end. I'm not involved in transactions or anything like that, but I have to keep a lid on the operation. As long as I list the salary as capers, I'll be in the clear with the law."

"And you'll be paying taxes on it, right?"

"Yep. Uncle Sam is gonna get his rightful share."

Suddenly tears came to Donna Sue's eyes. "Oh, Dwayne! You don't know how happy you've made me. You're so different from your wild days."

"I love you, Donna Sue."

She gazed at him. "What?"

"I said I love you," he stated. "A few weeks ago before I seen you at Dawson Construction, I woke up in the middle of the night and it hit me like a brick. All along I've been in love with you. And I was so sad that you had gotten away from me." He paused, noticing her expression of wide-eyed surprise. "I hope you can learn to love me, too, now that we're back together."

"Let's talk about this when we're sober."

"Sure," he said. "Say! How about if I get a membership in the Prairie Wind Golf and Tennis Club?"

Donna Sue shook her head. "I couldn't stand to go there, Dwayne. There're people who would look down on me."

"Well! I bet they won't after I've got the Wheeler Detective Agency all set up and running."

She nodded her agreement. "Yeah! That'll learn 'em, dern 'em!"

Donna Sue now could believe the changes in Dwayne were permanent. And he'd said he loved her. Dwayne had never made such a declaration in the past.

CHAPTER 14

F *rau* Griselde Schweitzer was nervous and confused.
   After the weekend with her mother and daughter, she had returned to the hotel lodgings she shared with Henry Hawkins. She expected to see him sometime that evening, but he failed to show up. After her grievous war experiences, she expected the worst. Black markets and other crimes were rampant in the still unsettled atmosphere of the defeated and divided German nation. Major Hawkins might have been shot or stabbed on some dark street.

   The next morning, she went to work hoping he would come in later. But after the passing of a couple of days, he still hadn't returned. Griselde continued to fetch his mail and other work documents and place them in his inbox.

   Another week passed and the director of the Bureau of Property Recovery called her to his office and inquired about both Hawkins and Bruno Schlagger's whereabouts. It was common knowledge in the organization that she and Hawkins cohabited as did several other stenographers and secretaries with managers. Griselde said she had no idea of the two men's whereabouts. The director didn't seem to believe her, giving the woman nervous feelings developed during the Nazi regime's existence.

"You are not in any trouble, *Frau* Schweitzer," he assured her. "But we are worried about the major and Schlagger. Perhaps something serious has happened. When did you last see either one of them?"

"I saw the major in the early afternoon several days ago," she said. "He told me he had an appointment and did not know when he would return. He gave me permission to take time off to visit my mother and daughter while he was gone. I have not seen him since."

"What about Schlagger?"

"I cannot recall the last time I talked with *Herr* Schlagger," she replied. "He and I do not converse very often."

"I see. Well, let us hope for the best. Perhaps they are dealing with some complicated matters."

"*Ja, Herr Direktor.*"

Another week passed and Griselde spent the weekend with her mother and daughter as usual. When she returned to the hotel Sunday evening, she anticipated seeing Major Hawkins. But he was a no-show once again.

———

ON THE FOLLOWING THURSDAY SHE WAS summoned back to the director's office. This time there were two men with him. One wore a U.S. Army uniform. The director said, "*Frau* Schweitzer, these gentlemen wish to speak to you regarding Major Harry Hawkins and Bruno Schlagger. This is *Oberstleutnant* Kobelski and *Herr* Arnsteiner."

Arnsteiner gave her a friendly smile and spoke in

German. "We simply have a few questions to ask you, *Frau* Schweitzer. It should not take long."

Despite his friendliness, Griselde was frightened out of her wits. Why were the two men looking for Major Hawkins? Why was one of them an American lieutenant colonel? Who was the other one? He was obviously a German. Now she was truly suspicious of her boss. What sort of trouble was he in? Or was it she that faced trouble?

The director spoke to the visitors. "There is a small conference room down the hall. You are welcome to use it." He turned to Griselde. "Please take them there, *Frau* Schweitzer."

She led them from the director's office down the hall a short way and opened the door to the room. There was a table with several chairs arranged around it. The American officer spoke for the first time after they were inside. "Shall we sit down and make ourselves comfortable?"

David Arnsteiner spoke up in German. "The *Oberstleutnant* suggests we sit down. I will act as a translator for him."

The officer pulled some papers from a briefcase he carried with him. "I see your husband is listed as missing in action."

The translated conversation began.

Griselde swallowed nervously and spoke in a low tone. "Yes. He was with the Sixth Army at Stalingrad."

"Do you recall when you received the last letter from him?"

"I think it was in late 1942," she answered. "I have it at home."

"Is your home in the hotel?"

Griselde shook her head. "I am only staying there. My home is with my mother and daughter who live in an apartment close by."

"I see," Colonel Kobelski said. "And you stay at the hotel with Major Hawkins, do you not?"

She blushed. "Yes."

"Are you lovers?"

"No...yes...no...what I mean is that he hired me as a secretary if I would live with him during the week. I am allowed to visit my mother and daughter on the weekends."

Arnsteiner spoke to Kobelski in English. "She is embarrassed, Roger. But this is a common thing. I am sure she is paid extra and that means it helps support her mother and daughter."

"I understand," Kobelski said. "I guess it's another hellish example of how war is worse for women and children. Especially the ones on the losing side. Ask her how much he pays her."

Arnsteiner asked the question.

"The major gives me fifteen dollars a week," Griselde said. "Sometimes more but never less. My pay from the Bureau is also fifteen dollars. I am paid in American money that I exchange for German marks at the U.S. bank down the street."

The statement surprised Arnsteiner. Once more he spoke to Kobelski. "That is odd. I know for a fact that the bureau only pays him thirty dollars per week. I can't see how he could give her half of it. Remember, he is not a real retired major from the British Army so he would have no pension. And I can tell you from my own experience, the British military pay is dismal."

"This situation is turning into a real mystery," Kobelski remarked. "Ask her to tell us what she knows about Hawkins, but don't let on he was using an alias."

Arnsteiner did as requested.

"He was a major in the British Army," Griselde

replied. "He is retired and was hired to work at the Bureau of Property Recovery by the American government."

"Has he spoken of a family? Is he married?" Kobelski inquired.

Griselde shrugged. "I know nothing of his personal life. And I never asked him to tell me about himself." She paused, then added, "He was always very kind and respectful toward me."

"Tell us about his work."

"He receives reports from the Bureau's activities in the hunt for property stolen from Jewish people," Griselde explained. "He passes it on to other offices to locate it."

"Did he have any particular interest in certain properties?" Arnsteiner asked.

"No," Griselde replied. Then she thought a moment. "He always wanted me to file any reports on art. Paintings mostly."

Now Arnsteiner was really interested. "What does he do with those files?"

"He sends them off."

"Who to?"

"I do not know," she answered. "He told me those were special cases and he had to hand deliver them. So once a week he would leave the office for an afternoon to take care of that business."

Arnsteiner realized she would know nothing more of the art files.

Kobelski asked, "Do you receive any money from the West German government in regards to your husband?"

"Only a mere stipend. I cannot get death benefits because he is officially listed as missing."

"What was his rank?"

"He was an *unteroffizier*," Griselde stated.

"I see. A corporal. So he wasn't in the *Waffen-SS*?"

Griselde shook her head. "He was not very soldierly. Before he was drafted into the Army he was a baker." She sighed. "He was also a baker in the Army and didn't serve on the frontlines."

Arnsteiner translated her answers for Kobelski adding, "Everybody was on the frontlines in the last days of the fighting at Stalingrad. He could very well have been killed or captured."

Kobelski turned to Griselde. "How well do you know Bruno Schlagger?"

"Not well at all."

"Do the major and Schlagger go out together often?" Kobelski inquired.

"No. Only a few times. I never know where they go."

Kobelski put his papers back in the briefcase. "I don't think the lady has any sort of information that would interest us. Go ahead and dismiss her, David."

Griselde wasted no time in leaving the room.

"We've got a hell of a job ahead of us," Kobelski said. "Finding the imposter in the present mass of secretive and criminal gangs is going to be near impossible. There is no doubt that this Schlagger guy is in on the fraudulent bastard's activities."

"I am going after both of them," Arnsteiner said. "I shall ask the director here for their file photographs."

"Good luck," Kobelski said. "Well, I must get back to my office. If I run across anything that would interest you I'll contact you through Yitzhak Cohen."

CHAPTER 15

The *Wolflager*—Wolf Lair—was the name given the stone house hidden among a thick stand of spruce trees in an isolated area in the West German state of Bavaria. It was also the name of the organization that used it as a headquarters. This was done in spite of its cover up as a convalescent hospital for former soldiers.

The members of the *Wolflager* were veterans of the fanatic *Waffen-SS* units that began as bodyguards for Adolf Hitler and were later expanded into a hard-fighting independent Nazi army. But unlike normal fraternal military societies, the *Wolflager* was an illegal active duty combat and intelligence unit with several nefarious goals. Circumstances, however, caused most of their operations to concentrate on clandestine activities to build up their strength and capabilities for future armed revolutions. This included developing a solid financial base to pay for their grandiose plans.

They were under the command of Franz Taubert, a former *Waffen-SS gruppenführer*. This was the equivalent rank of lieutenant general. Due to the lack of senior officers in the *Wolflager*, Taubert's second-in-command was a *Waffen-SS-standartenführer*. His name was Manfred von Leipinger.

There was also one member of the Wolflager who was not a former *Waffen-SS* soldier. This was fifteen-year-old Herbert Hock. He had been one of the members of the Hitler Youth aged fourteen to sixteen called to active duty during the last desperate days of the Nazi reign. He and other boys were assigned to combat units. They had already had received military training in their association, so it was feasible to immediately transfer them to the frontlines.

When Herbert and his pals arrived at their assigned infantry unit they were placed at a roadblock outside their hometown of Sommerfeld with orders to stop the approaching American forces. They dug in and simply waited to see what would happen. Late that afternoon American soldiers appeared to their direct front, slowly and vigilantly moving toward the town. The boys, armed with only bolt-action Mauser rifles, immediately opened fire. The Americans pulled back and the youngsters congratulated themselves. It looked like they could report mission completed when their commander returned.

Then things suddenly turned into a roaring, exploding hell for the youngsters.

Mortar shells rained down on them and in less than three minutes they were all killed except young Herbert Hock. He was badly wounded and taken prisoner after the Americans advanced to mop up further resistance.

The wounded kid was turned over to a medical unit to be taken by ambulance to a prisoner of war camp's hospital. Weeks later, when the Germans surrendered, he was released to go home because of his age and physical condition.

Herbert arrived traumatized and grief-stricken at his parents' house. They were overjoyed to see that their youngest boy had survived combat. His older brother had been a gunner on a bomber in the *Luftwaffe* who was killed during the Battle of Britain. To add to their bad luck, they were now destitute because his father's print shop had been blown to hell under the fierce pounding of numerous artillery barrages.

Bruno Schlagger knew the family and got permission from Manfred von Leipinger to let the boy work at the *Wolflager* outside Munich as a janitor to reward his service in combat. He received a small salary that he took home to his parents in Sommerfeld every week.

Herbert also had enough sense not to complain about what had happened to him in those final awful days of the war. Instead, in order to hold on to the job he and his family needed so desperately, he gave the impression of being proud to have served in combat against the overwhelming American Army.

The boy worked at his job under the impression he was employed in a hospital. However, he was forbidden to enter certain parts of the building to perform his janitorial duties. Herbert was puzzled by the rule, but his training in the highly disciplined Hitler Youth had conditioned him to obey orders without asking questions.

———

THE *WAFFEN-SS* UNITS HAD NOTHING TO DO with the concentration camps. Those criminal activities were carried on by the *Allgemeine-SS*. However, the *Waffen-SS* committed their own share of war crimes. The majority of these offenses was the shooting of prisoners of war that occurred when it was difficult or impossible to transport them to prison camps.

Taubert and several other surviving high-ranking *Waffen-SS* officers had been the first to realize that Nazi Germany was going to lose the war. While showing a pseudo-confident attitude toward their troops to keep them fighting, these commanders of large units made serious plans to renew the war after the cessation of hostilities. That meant they had to make sure certain that reliable sub-commanders would survive those last days of desperate fighting. For that reason, they issued orders to certain trusted leaders to surrender to the Americans during the closing days of the conflict. This was because they would have been summarily executed if captured by the Russians.

Waffen-SS Standartenführer Manfred von Leipinger was one the chosen few.

The high-ranking commanding generals also knew that they would need massive amounts money to raise an army and renew Hitler's aim of a thousand-year *Reich*. Taubert and his ilk were aware of gold, money and priceless works of art that had been looted from the occupied nations by high Nazi officials. These items were stolen from museums, banks, government buildings and other places where valuable items were either stored or on display. Another source of this treasure was the homes of wealthy Jews who had been sent off to the death camps.

All this was hidden away in scattered locations. Secret teams of especially chosen *Waffen-SS* officers and soldiers were formed to ferret out these locations and haul the goods away to new hiding places. Sometimes members of the *Allgemeine-SS* who had originally collected the loot resisted those raids. They were quickly eliminated with intense prejudice.

Now, in the early postwar years, the leaders and troopers of the *Wolflager* were the central custodians of this "liberated" plunder. And it was Franz Taubert who was in charge of raising money by selling off those spoils of war.

———

NIGEL HAWTHORNE ALIAS MAJOR HENRY HAWKINS was a trusted ally of the *Wolflager*. His illegal dealings in the black market, the counterfeit of German military scrip and other profitable criminal activities had attracted the attention of high ranking officials of the West German police. They had tried to prosecute him numerous times, but he always slipped through their fingers with bribes, threats and murder.

Finally, commissioner of police Werner Ullmann, who was a member of the *Wolflager*, arranged a secret meeting with Hawthorne to see about the sale of expensive paintings. Ullmann was aware Hawthorne was an expert in such situations. The disgraced Englishman knew the people who would have the skills and desires to participate in that type of criminal dealings. The German police commissioner and the British wheeler-dealer formed an arrangement between themselves. Ullmann sent subtle secret orders down the various law enforcement echelons to cease all cases involving Nigel Hawthorne.

Hawthorne proved to be a valuable asset to the *Wolflager*. He first assumed the identity of a retired British Army officer of the Grenadier Guards he had known before his court-martial and conviction for embezzlement. This was Henry Hawkins. The retired officer would not be on current British military rosters, and the fact he had died guaranteed nobody would know about his existence, or lack thereof in defeated Germany.

With that impressive cover, Hawthorne wrangled a position in the Bureau of Property Recovery. He altered his appearance and concentrated on valuable works of art with a clever scheme of hiding them in America prior to selling them to unscrupulous art dealers and collectors elsewhere in the world.

At that point in the setup, Hawthorne needed a distribution center. And what better location for that activity than the United States? He knew of two reliable Americans who could handle the job. Those were Peter Van Dyke and Dwayne Wheeler who had both been very helpful in the German military scrip swindle. This complicated criminal conspiracy had been a rousing success.

However, it was vital that Wheeler be kept in the dark about the truth of the present operation. Thus, Hawthorne concocted a scheme about a cabal of wealthy art collectors who traded paintings among themselves. He organized an operational procedure of registered mailings of art to Wichita, Kansas U.S.A. for distribution when that part of the plot was put into operation. He also set up generous pay and bonuses to encourage Wheeler to maintain a deep dedication to the project. Such amounts of money would also discourage the private detective from wanting to get out of the project in case he somehow learned the truth. If that happened and the American refused to continue his participation, then arrangements would have to be made to silence him.

CHAPTER 16

It was early Friday evening and Donna Sue had just parked the Buick outside her apartment house and entered the building. She was in her usual good mood at that time of the week. She knew Dwayne would be waiting for her and they would have a fun evening going to the Homestyle Restaurant and then a movie. And of course there would be two nights of sleeping together during the weekend.

Her entrance into the apartment brought on the usual expressions of affection between them, then Dwayne stepped back with a wide grin. "I got good news, toots. Pete Van Dyke and Sybil are in town. Pete left a message with my answering service and I gave 'em a call. They want us to go over to their suite in the Riverside Hotel for a few drinks and a room service meal. Then we'll all head over to the Roadhouse for an evening of fun and dancing. They've already made reservations."

"Wonderful!" Donna Sue exclaimed, her excitement increased over the prospect of going to the night club. "I was wondering why you were wearing your blue suit. I'll hurry up and take a bath and get into my glad rags."

"We'll have a real good time. I told 'em we're back together, so they want to make a celebration of it."

Donna Sue hurried into the bedroom to begin her preparations for a special evening. Dwayne sat down on the sofa to wait, turning on the radio to a local disk jockey who played the latest swing songs of the big bands. The shamus could hear Donna Sue happily humming as she laid out her evening clothes before bathing.

———

THE VAN DYKES HAD BEEN ABLE TO RENT SUITE 206 once more. The accommodation was their favorite at the Riverside Hotel. Pete always considered it good luck when they scored that particular lodging when in Wichita. He glanced over at Sybil and laughed aloud. "I can't wait to present Dwayne with the surprise."

"He'll be so pleased," Sybil said. "Are you going to give it to him right away?"

"I'll wait until after we've served the first round of drinks."

Sybil had neatly arranged the liquor, mixes and glasses in the sitting room for the event. "I don't remember Donna Sue's preference in cocktails or wine."

"I believe wine would be her choice."

"In that case I'll be prepared to share the chardonnay with her. And if she wants a mixed drink I'm ready for that, too."

"Dwayne and I always enjoy straight scotch," Pete said. "But his favorite liquor is one of the Jack Daniels variety. I was going to order some, but I wasn't sure if I'd get the right one."

"Dwayne will be happy with scotch. He always is."

The whirring of the elevator coming to a stop down the hall could be heard. Pete went over to the door and looked out to see Dwayne and Donna Sue emerging from the conveyance. "There you are! Hello, you two!" He stepped back to let the guests enter the suite.

Pete kissed Donna Sue on the cheek and shook hands with Dwayne. The shamus, although getting plenty of loving from Donna Sue, still enjoyed the peck Sybil allowed him on her lips.

Dwayne glanced over at Pete. "So what brings you back to Wichita?"

"We simply wanted to have a few drinks with you and Donna Sue. And speaking of libations, what're your pleasures?"

"We'll take whatever you guys are having."

"All right then," Pete announced. "Chardonnay for the ladies and scotch neat for the gentlemen." He went over to the sideboard and prepared the drinks. With that done, he handed Donna Sue and Sybil their glasses and held out a tumbler of the whiskey for Dwayne before picking up his own. He raised it. "The first item on the agenda is a toast to the renewal of your romance. May it last an eternity."

"Hear! Hear!" Sybil called out.

Pete suggested, "Shall we sit?" They all settled down on the plush furniture and he gave Dwayne a cheerful glance. "Now I'll let you in on another reason for our visit here. The cabal is happy with your work, my lad. In fact —" He reached inside his jacket pocket and pulled out an envelope. "—here is a sincere expression of that appreciation."

Dwayne took the small package and opened it. "Jesus!

Five one-hunnerd dollar bills! I don't know if I deserve that much of a bonus."

"Sure you do," Pete countered. "Everything is going smoothly on your end of the operation. Dwayne, you're a real down to earth guy, and I think that's a big advantage for you. It conceals your very creative intellect that benefits you quite well at times. And this has been one of those times."

Donna Sue reached over and patted Dwayne's hand. "He really is so different than he used to be. I guess we all know that he's gotten himself into some pretty shady deals now and then in the past."

"Well, not to worry, Donna Sue," Pete said. "This cabal thing is a legitimate enterprise."

"I'm so glad. He's even planning on enlarging his private detective business."

Dwayne made an affirmative nod. "And this bonus is gonna be a big help."

Pete was interested. "What've you got in mind, Dwayne?"

"I want to be able to get a larger and more impressive office to begin with. Then I'll hire a couple of operatives. Prob'ly retired cops. After that I'll expand farther into security projects of hired guards and that sort of thing."

"Good for you, Dwayne!" Sybil exclaimed.

Pete took a deep swallow of his scotch. "It's too bad the Roadhouse doesn't serve meals. I arranged an eight o'clock reservation at the club, so we'd better order room service now." He got up and took some menus off the radio and passed them around. "Choose what you want, folks. I'll call in the orders."

———

FORTY MINUTES LATER, WITH THE SUPPERS reduced to dirty dishes, they went down to the hotel lobby and walked over to valet parking. Dwayne handed his ticket to a driver who trotted off to get his vehicle. When the guy returned with a 1948 Nash Suburban station wagon, Pete let out a long whistle of admiration.

"It looks to me like you're already near attaining your goals, Dwayne."

"I made a few bucks and didn't put down any bets on the ponies. This woody was the one luxury I allowed myself before beginning a strict management of my funds."

When all were in the roomy vehicle, Dwayne drove off the hotel lot onto Douglas and turned north on Broadway, heading for Arkansas Avenue.

———

JACK WALLACE AND DENNY TARBALL, MANNING the Roadhouse doors, greeted the four in their usual happy and courteous manner. Dwayne *et al* entered and presented themselves to the maître 'd. That worthy persona checked them off the reservations list and snapped his finger to summon a waitress.

Drinks were ordered and the four settled into the ambiance of the activity around them. After a few moments, Pete took Sybil's hand and led her out on the dance floor. At the end of the song they remained for another whirl around the room. At that point Dwayne and Donna Sue joined them.

It had all the beginnings of a wonderful evening. Four very happy people looking forward to bountiful futures.

CHAPTER 17

Lieutenant Colonel Roger Kobelski, United States Army Military Intelligence, sat at his desk studying the two photos of the bogus Major Harry Hawkins. He had acquired them from the Bureau of Property Recovery. The Englishman was shown front and right sides in the likenesses.

Yitzhak Cohen and David Arnsteiner were seated across from him. He provided each with a set of the two photographs. "Well," the lieutenant colonel said. "Have you guys been able to discover any disguises in these portraits?"

Arnsteiner dropped his photos on the desk after giving them a close scrutiny. "I would say the eyebrows and that moustache are false. But that's just a guess. I wish they had used a better class of cameras for I.D. shots."

"I agree," Cohen remarked. "It is indeed hard to tell if his appearance is fake or not. His hair is rather thick along the sides. If one cut that back and removed the eyebrows and moustache he'd look quite different."

"I knew he was definitely an upper class Brit the first

time I met him," Arnsteiner said. "That crowd has a definite enjoyment of putting on theatrical performances. As schoolboys and university students their academies of learning perform skits and plays quite often. The British officers we had over us in the Jewish Brigade were from the middle and working class, but they did the same types of programs at unit parties when we were pulled out of the line. Some even played female parts in women's clothing."

Kobelski chuckled. "I'd be afraid to dress up like a female in the midst of troops just back from a combat area."

Arnsteiner grinned. "I will admit that some of them did seem a bit appealing at the time."

"That gives me an idea," Cohen said. "The *Tsad'yod-mem* also has an intelligence branch. And they have a very talented sketch artist who is skillful when it comes to portraits. Perhaps he could copy these photos with normal eyebrows, no moustache and shorter hair."

Kobelski was impressed. "Ah, yes! The *Tsad'yod-mem* —A.K.A. the Hunters in English. All right, Yitzhak, take a set of these photos and see what your artists can do with both poses."

"We shall be back with the sketches as soon as possible," Cohen promised as he and Arnsteiner left the office.

———

DWAYNE AND DONNA SUE REMAINED ELATED BY his plans to become a big shot shamus commanding a private police department. And the five hundred dollar bonus Pete Van Dyke had presented him added to their good moods.

On the Friday a week after the Van Dykes' visit, they

followed their usual tradition of getting together at her apartment then going to the Home-style Restaurant to dine. After the meal, they went to the Orpheum Theater and enjoyed *The Third Man* with Orson Welles and Joseph Cotton. Most of the time they would have gone straight back to Dwayne's apartment for lovemaking, but the zither music in the movie stimulated them enough to take a ride around the city, going up to Riverside Park and all the way down to the Wichita Municipal Airport.

Now, back in his apartment, they had just made love and were sitting up against the headboard of the bed, smoking cigarettes. Dwayne exhaled smoke, saying, "That five hunnerd dollars cash money is gonna come in handy, but it'll take a bit of doing to sneak it into the bank account."

"I wish I had that kind of a problem. By the way, what bank have you chosen to deal with?"

"The Kansas Merchant and Farmers Bank," he replied. "I deposited a thousand bucks into a checking account and another grand into a savings program."

"How did you cover the source of the money?"

"I've typed up invoices of nonexistent minor capers," he replied. "Surveillance, keeping a lookout for shoplifters, checking references and stuff like that."

"Won't the I.R.S. look into those?"

"They never have before. I'm allowed by law to keep my clients' names confidential, so I don't have to identify nobody on the paperwork."

"You don't have to identify *any*body on the paper-work," she corrected him.

"Gotcha, toots. So if they wanted to check things closer they'd have to get court warrants. The amount I show as earned is so minor they won't bother unless there's a crime involved." He snuffed out his cigarette in the ashtray on the nightstand, and was silent for several long moments.

"Something on your mind?" she asked.

"Yeah." He hesitated, then said, "I want us to get married."

She glared at him. "Now that's a real romantic proposal."

"I ain't feeling romantic 'cause I know you're gonna say no."

"How do you know I'm gonna say no?"

Dwayne sighed, then leaned over and kissed her lightly on the mouth. "Donna Sue, I'm in love with you and want you. Will you marry me?"

"Yes."

He was dumbfounded. "Oh? I mean, oh! I mean that's great. It really is. When d'you wanna do it?"

"I think we should wait until after you get everything settled on expanding your business," she counseled. "And I agree you shouldn't hire me as your receptionist."

"Really?"

"Yes, *really*. I think you should hire me as your office manager."

"I don't want my wife to work!"

"Look, Dwayne. I don't mind doing it and I have a lot of business skills. Once the loan officers see that you're cost-conscious enough to use me, they'll be more impressed with your project."

"Okay, that's a good idea," he acknowledged. "But after things are rolling along good I want you to quit."

"We'll have to talk a little more about this subject later."

"Uh oh!"

CHAPTER 18

WAC Corporal Barb Carey was at her desk bringing Lieutenant Colonel Kobelski's Rolodex up to date. The twenty-eight-year-old was plumpish with bright blue eyes and auburn hair. Several of the enlisted men had tried to take her out, but she never accepted those requests for dates. This gave the impression to her fellow office workers that she was a bit stuck up as well as fully dedicated to her job.

David Arnsteiner and Yitzhak Cohen appeared at her duty station and interrupted her Rolodex task. Arnsteiner stated, "Good morning. We are here as per Colonel Kobelski's request."

The sergeant pressed the intercom to her boss's' office. "Sir. Mister Cohen and Mister Arnsteiner are here."

"Send them in."

The two Jews presented themselves and Cohen immediately dropped several photostats on Kobelski's desk. These were the artist's altered sketch of the phony Major Henry Hawkins.

"Here it is," Cohen said. "He looks quite a bit different, does he not?"

"He sure as hell does," Kobelski agreed.

Arnsteiner stated, "If I have ever seen an upper class snobbish Englishman, there he is in all his glory."

Kobelski asked, "Are these for me?"

"Certainly," Cohen said. "By the way, you may have a bit of trouble contacting me for awhile. Some difficulties have popped up in our procedures that I must tend to."

"Perfectly understandable."

Arnsteiner added, "And I have my own agenda to follow that will keep me busy. But I shall be available when and if needed."

"Of course," Kobelski said. "I recall you mentioned your interest in recovering valuables stolen from Jewish families."

"It's personal with me," Arnsteiner revealed. "There were five valuable old masterpiece paintings that were taken from my boyhood home. The house has since been returned to me and I want to recover the artwork and replace them on that same wall where they belong."

"Well, I certainly wish you luck in your various activities, gentlemen," Kobelski said.

"Thank you, Roger," Cohen replied. "We will check in with you later. Let us hope we are able to identify the mysterious Englishman, eh?"

The visitors left the office and Kobelski looked at the drawings, wondering how accurate they might be. He remembered seeing likenesses in newspapers of criminal suspects drawn by police artists. Unfortunately, when the felons were arrested, none resembled the illustrations even faintly. He hoped these were more accurate. He planned to send a set to the Grenadier Guards Headquarters at Buckingham Palace. If it turned out that no one recognized the imposter, that would mean he hadn't belonged to that regiment. Kobelski would have to put out an all-points bulletin through the Allies' military intelligence bureaus. That would make it time consuming to capture the criminal.

Kobelski pressed the intercom button to summon his WAC secretary. "Sergeant Carey, I need to have a package prepared to send to London right away."

———

ROGER KOBELSKI SYMPATHIZED WITH YITZHAK Cohen about his desire to establish a Jewish State. But he did not share the man's enthusiasm. Kobelski's roots were deep in America and very meaningful to him. He was descended from a young Polish Jew who had traveled across Europe on foot back in the 18th Century going all the way to Great Britain. His name was Avigdor Kobelski and he was fleeing the massacres suffered by his people in countless pogroms committed by anti-Semitic Polish and Russian mobs. When he landed in England he couldn't speak English but had the address of a small Jewish neighborhood in Portsmouth.

Avigdor was helped by the Jewish community and found employment in a chandler's shop on the docks. After two years of dealing with shipping companies he learned to speak fluent English even though he had a noticeable accent. Eventually Avigdor heard about opportunities in the thirteen colonies across the North Atlantic. It seemed like a good opportunity to get farther away from European bigots. He quickly booked passage for the New World.

The ambitious youth went to work in a shipping company's office in Boston. He had a natural bent for commerce and rose up quickly through the staff until he was named chief clerk. Avigdor married a pretty Jewish girl named Sadie and purchased a comfortable home in a middle-class neighborhood. He and Sadie prospered and raised a family of five children.

Twenty uneventful but comfortable years passed, then a great turbulence swept through the area when the American Revolution broke out. Their oldest son Asa joined a Massachusetts regiment and fought in the cause for Independence. When the war ended he was a captain and company commander.

Thus began a line of American soldiers throughout the Kobelski generations. They served in every war over the decades, and were proud of being officers while fighting for the causes of the United States. The Kobelskis were not a particularly religious clan, being bitter about the treatment of their forbears by Russians and Poles. By the time Lieutenant Colonel Roger Kobelski was born in 1915 he was only 35 percent Jewish due to Kobelski men constantly intermarrying with Gentiles over the years.

Roger was the first of his family to attend West Point and become a military professional. Now, in postwar Germany, he had been infuriated by the Nazis' persecution of Jews since he felt a kindred connection to the victims. He hoped they would be able to establish their goal of a homeland in Palestine.

But the lieutenant colonel had no interest in participating in that cause. He also wished success to David Arnsteiner in his quest to find the property of Jews who had died in the concentration camps. He happily donated money to both efforts, but that was as far as he would go. Roger Kobelski was an American and that was that.

———

HERBERT HOCK, THE FORMER NAZI YOUTH soldier, limped through the offices and rooms of the *Wolflager*, emptying wastebaskets into his trash cart to be taken down to the incinerator in the cellar for burning. This task, plus his other janitorial duties, gave him the opportunity to move easily throughout those parts of the building where he was allowed.

The youngster eased the cart down the wooden staircase to the earthen floor, then wheeled it over to the incinerator. This was a daily job since his employers didn't want any loose papers lying around the building. Herbert shoveled coal into the interior of the device then laid kindling on top. After lighting the wood sticks and giving the fire a chance to build up, he began removing the paper from the cart one piece at a time. He carefully scanned each one before tossing it into the flames. He came across one document that caught his attention. He carefully folded it and stuck it in his pocket.

When the burning chore was completed, Herbert pulled the cart back up the steps and pushed it over to the storage cabinet where he kept the brooms and mops. His day's work was done and he checked in with Bruno Schlagger at a desk in the hallway.

The boy asked, "Is there anything else for me to do?"

Schlagger looked up from a magazine he was reading. This was the main interior guard station of the building and was manned as per a rotation roster. He picked up the duty sheet and checked out the assignments on it. "*Nein*, Herbert. All is well. You may go home now."

"*Danke, Herr* Schlagger."

The boy went out the front door and took his bike off the porch. He got on it and began peddling down the road toward Sommerfeld where he lived with his parents.

HERBERT HOCK DETESTED THE *WAFFEN-SS* MEN he worked for. Although those objects of this hatred respected him for his war service, Herbert had his own opinions of the last days of the conflict.

When he and the other Hitler Youth lads were assigned at the roadblock by a *Waffen-SS* officer, they were told to stop the advancing Americans until reinforcements could come up and help them. When the Americans reached their position, they were held up by the boys who fired at them with rifles, waiting for reinforcements. But no help arrived as the Americans set up their mortar squads and fired shells into the midst of the youngsters. All were killed but Herbert and after the war he realized the officer had lied to them. There was no back-up coming. They had been sacrificed to slow down the Americans long enough for the *Waffen-SS* troops to withdraw to better defensive positions.

Herbert didn't think the sacrifice was so honorable. To him it had all been a cruel deception. And he was going to get his revenge come hell or high water.

WHEN HERBERT BIKED INTO TOWN, THE STREETS of Sommerfeld were filled with people going home for the evening. He went down the main boulevard to the market area, pedaling to a store that bore a sign reading **DISPLACED PERSONS REGISTRATION OFFICE**. He walked inside where a young woman was seated at a desk.

"Hello, Herbert. Do you have something for us?"

"Yes," he said, reaching into his pants pocket. He

pulled out the document he had kept from the incinerator. "Please give this to *Herr* Cohen."

"I shall do that, Herbert. Thank you."

A couple of months before, when Herbert figured out that the *Wolflager* was not really a hospital, he took some of the documents he thought might be important to the registration office for information. The boy hoped the helpful people there might have connections with organizations who could use them against the Nazis. He, of course, didn't realize this was a front for Jewish anti-Nazi activities, and Yitzhak Cohen assured him that they would see that the papers were given to the proper authorities who could make good use of them.

Thus every time Herbert found something that seemed part of a wicked plot, he showed up at the registration office with the evidence.

CHAPTER 19

The Jews of *Tsad'yod-mem*—The Hunters—knew all about the neo-Nazi *Waffen-SS*, their operations and the exact location of the *Wolflager*. Every bit of this essential intelligence had been given them by young Herbert Hock. However, Cohen and his people wisely refrained from taking any overt action against these enemies. At that particular time, it was more prudent to let the Nazis carry on with their nefarious activities in order to discover more hiding places of looted riches. There was also the possibility of locating Nazi agents who had infiltrated government bureaus and offices. Dealing with such individuals would require skillful and careful observation to avoid alerting the fanatical Aryans.

———

DAVID ARNSTEINER STEPPED INTO YITZHAK Cohen's office the day after Herbert's delivery of the *Wolflager* document. He was responding to a summons that he delay all his present activities, and meet with the man. Arnsteiner had his own agenda and was more than a little irritated at being interrupted in his work.

"What is going on, Yitzhak?" he asked, sitting down. He checked his watch. "Will this take much time?"

Cohen grinned at him. "This is going to take as much time as I want it to take."

"You seem happy."

"And you are about to be as happy as I," Cohen said. He slid the document delivered by Herbert across the table.

Arnsteiner perused the text that had been rescued from the incinerator. When he finished, he looked up at Cohen. "I cannot believe this!"

"It is amazing," Cohen agreed. "And it fits right in with your hunt for stolen paintings."

"It seems confusing, but I see the wisdom of it," Arnsteiner remarked. "They are shipping the paintings to America before having them dispatched from there to other places."

"Exactly! That means there are various locations where the items are being hidden until sold," Cohen said. He turned his attention back to the document. "The American destination is Wichita. A city in Kansas, I believe. I checked for the location in my world atlas. It is located almost geometrically in the center of America. So here is what will happen. I shall make further investigations into this intelligence and get back to you. In the meantime, carry on as usual."

Arnsteiner stood up. "This is great news! *Buvakasha!* Please! Hurry up the process, my friend."

"Of course," Cohen said. "The sooner we wrap this up, the sooner we can begin assassinating Nazis."

———

DWAYNE AND DONNA SUE SAT AT THEIR USUAL booth in the Homestyle Restaurant. After being served, she took a drink of ice tea, giving Dwayne a meaningful look. "We have to talk."

His eyes opened wide in dreadful surprise. "Are you breaking up with me?"

"Of course not. The fact is I have been giving some very serious consideration to our plans to establish your expansion of the detective agency. I think this evening should be devoted to me explaining some ideas that have popped into *my* mind. That means we won't be going to the movies."

"That's fine," Dwayne said. "But what about—"

Donna Sue interrupted, "We can make love after the confab. So get that little boy pout off your face. This is going to be important. And it involves how you should handle your monetary activities from here on. Don't worry. I am only adding and tweaking your own ideas."

His attitude changed to one of genuine interest. Dwayne had the utmost trust and confidence in Donna Sue when it came to her opinions and calculations. The shamus had learned she was smarter and more sensible and prudent than he.

"I think you should be my office manager for sure," Dwayne said.

"That is exactly part of my plans."

———

AN HOUR LATER THE NASH HAD BEEN PUT IN THE parking garage and they were walking down Market Street toward the apartment house. Dwayne asked, "Are you sure we can't hop into bed first?"

She looked at him with an expression that he knew

meant that particular idea would receive no consideration. The couple went to his digs and Donna Sue carried her suitcase into the bedroom while Dwayne got the wine and Jack Daniels whiskey ready.

He sat down and Donna Sue joined him on the sofa. "Okay," she announced. "I have been giving considerable thought to how you're going to use the money hidden here in the apartment to finance the projects. As I told you at the restaurant, it is heavily based on your own basic plans that you have discussed. So! What you are going to have to do is what is called money laundering. In other words, you're going to take ill-gotten gains and sneak them into circulation."

"They wasn't all ill-gotten. I got seven hunnerd and fifty bucks of that money from the F.B.I."

"Really? What was that all about?"

"I can't talk about it and it's best you don't know," Dwayne cautioned her. "There's also another seven hunnerd and fifty that *are* what you'd call ill-gotten. But I swear to you it was used for a good cause. And you'd approve what I did if you knew what it was all about."

"All right," Donna Sue said. "That's not enough to raise suspicion from the I.R.S. anyhow. So here's how we start out. You go to the bank and deposit an additional fifteen hundred dollars in the savings account. Then I'll write out a business expansion proposal and you take it to the bank for submission to a loan officer. From that point on you can pay off the loan with the rest of the money you have here in the apartment."

"I get it! I get rid of the dough by slipping it into a bank who'll use it in their investments and loans, right?"

"Right. Now tell me about the two hundred dollars a week you're being paid by those art collectors."

"I get paid ever' two weeks," Dwayne explained. "Pete

Van Dyke sends me four one hunnerd dollar money orders. He's gotta do it that way since that's the maximum for a single order. He says it's either that or Western Union. And Western Union is not the best place in the world for secrecy."

Donna Sue was thoughtful for a moment. "And you're making phony invoices paid you by nonexistent clients to cover those payments. It's all listed as cash transactions, correct?"

"Yeah. You see it ain't unusual for a shamus to be paid in cash since some customers don't want any record of paying us for confidential investigations."

"Now here's a way to add about several thousand dollars to the kitty. I have a lot of jewelry Brian gave me. I can sell it all, then report that my apartment was burgled. That will keep us in the clear."

"You don't have to do that," Dwayne protested. "Why don't you hang on to them goodies?'

"I won't keep anything from that son of a bitch Brian Murchison," she growled. "I want everything about him out of my life. I believe you know a fence, right?"

"Sure. Pete Driscoll. He's the guy that gave me the evidence that solved Stub Durham's murder."

"Wonderful! Now we have to make it look like somebody broke into my apartment."

"I know how to do that," Dwayne said. "And if the cops ask you anything, tell 'em you think your old boyfriend Brian Murchison is behind it. They'll grill you pretty good, but stick to your story. The D.A. won't even investigate it after that. The Murchison family is pretty powerful in Wichita. He wouldn't dare even ask 'em anything about paying to have a burglary done." He lit a cigarette. "But I don't think you're gonna get a big payoff from Driscoll. He's gonna have to break the pieces up and all that. But I can make him give you at least half that much."

"Do it, Dwayne. And I have a question. Can you identify your customers on the invoices as 'Client A' and 'Client B, etcetera?"

"Sure. That wouldn't be any problem. My customers have a lawful right to privacy and I have an obligation to provide it for them."

"Good. There's really no reason to worry about the I.R.S. as long as you keep getting paid with postal money orders. That money and anything else you earn can be fed into your bank account for making loan payments. It's a sure thing you won't attract any attention from either the Federal or Kansas tax administrators."

"Then ever'thing's settled," he said. "Now can we go to bed?"

"I think that's a reasonable request."

CHAPTER 20

Lieutenant Colonel Roger Kobelski looked over his desktop at David Arnsteiner and Yitzhak Cohen. He folded his arms across his chest and leaned back in his chair. His face showed angry astonishment. "How in the hell did you people get hold of this information?"

Cohen shrugged. "We cannot divulge that, Roger. But it is irrefutably accurate and up to date."

"I'm sure it is," Kobelski said, taking another look at the photostat of the document they had just shown him. "A neo-Nazi organization—which you will not name—is dispatching stolen works of art by first sending them to America, huh?"

"Right," Arnsteiner said. "To Wichita, Kansas in America. From there they go into a distribution system of some sort. We have yet to discover what it is or how it works."

"And you want me to arrange for the F.B.I. to not only investigate this situation, but hand over any intelligence they acquire to you. You guys are getting kind of pushy, aren't you?"

"We have very good reasons, Roger," Cohen explained. "We are going to move against the Nazis when the time is right. But since the time is *not* right, we need help in order to find out all the facts and figures of their methodology. I believe that one time you mentioned you had a counterpart in the F.B.I. office here in Germany."

"That's right. And what about you? What sort of organization are you talking about that can eliminate neo-Nazis?"

Cohen replied, "All I can tell you is that it is Jewish."

Arnsteiner interjected, "We know the F.B.I. is conducting highly classified investigations into neo-Nazism here in Germany. We promise that if they help us with this, we will aid them in their efforts. And I believe I can safely say that at this time we have considerably more knowledge on the subject than they do."

"No doubt of that," Kobelski warily agreed. "But be forewarned that the F.B.I. does not like to become involved in situations without being able to establish an advantage for themselves. And that includes taking over the supervision and strategy completely."

Cohen was angry. "Did I not state that we would work with them in the future?"

"All right," Kobelski said. "I will contact their office in Munich and set up a meeting for you. Let me further inform you that they're a complicated intelligence bureaucracy and thorough as hell."

"We shall keep that in mind," Cohen promised.

———

DWAYNE WHEELER GOT OUT OF HIS STATION wagon, taking a brand new leather briefcase with him. He was lucky enough to get a parking place only a half a block down the street from the Kansas Merchant and Farmers Bank. He entered the building and sighted a sign indicating a loan desk. He walked over noting the nameplate identifying the man behind it.

EDGAR WHITTINGTON
LOAN OFFICER

"Hello, Mister Whittington," Dwayne greeted him. "I'm Dwayne Wheeler."

"Ah, yes!" Whittington said with a friendly grin. "My eleven o'clock. And right on time. Please sit down."

"Thanks," Dwayne said, setting the briefcase on the desk. He opened it and pulled out a sheaf of typed papers prepared by Donna Sue. "I'm obviously here to apply for a loan. A business loan." He handed the papers to Whittington.

"Yes. And I see that you deposited an additional fifteen hundred dollars into your savings account with us last week. How much do you wish to borrow?"

"Ten thousand dollars. I'm in the preparation phase of enlarging my business."

"Which is a private investigation office, correct?"

"Yes, sir! The Wheeler Detective Agency."

"We've taken the liberty of looking into your background. Very impressive, Mister Wheeler. You've solved some murders here in Wichita and have managed what appears to be an aboveboard operation. Of course there were those articles about you in the paper a couple of months or so back. The first said you were under scrutiny and might lose your state license. Then a later article appeared stating you were completely cleared of any wrongdoing and were able to renew your business."

"That was really embarrassing."

"On the contrary, Mister Wheeler. It shows us you've been thoroughly investigated and found in complete compliance with Federal and state laws. That is truly in your favor." He picked up the papers Dwayne had provided. "Ah, yes! You say you'll need ten thousand dollars. Mmm. It indicates you to want to hire an office manager and another detective. And obtain a new, larger office. Also two automobiles. Lastly there's a list of minor expenses." He looked up. "This is one of the best applications I've had the pleasure to work with. All carefully itemized with the expenses for each entry."

"That was done by my future office manager," Dwayne said. "She's also my future wife."

"Well!" Whittington chuckled. "That's certainly a convenient arrangement."

"She told me that it's best tax-wise for her to be put on a salary basis," Dwayne explained.

"And she is absolutely correct," Whittington stated. "This ten thousand dollar loan can be approved under certain conditions. We would like you to put an additional two thousand dollars in that savings account. Then don't touch it. That's your collateral. In fact, we'll put a freeze on the deposit. You do have some black marks on your credit rating. But they are minor things involving rents."

"I can understand that," Dwayne said agreeably. "There have been times in the past when things were tough for me. But I've gone far beyond that now."

"Indeed you have. As soon as that additional deposit is made, we'll have the paperwork prepared to advance you a ten thousand dollar loan at the usual commercial interest rate."

Dwayne closed his briefcase, stood up and offered his hand to Whittington. "I'll take care of that extra deposit right away."

The middle-aged bank guard in the lobby gave Dwayne a grin and salute as the shamus practically skipped to the door. Now he had to burglarize Donna Sue's apartment and "steal" her jewelry. Then he'd have to take it to Pete Driscoll to sell it. But there was no hurry to carry out that scheme.

———

TWO WEEKS HAD PASSED SINCE DAVID Arnsteiner and Yitzhak Cohen had visited Lieutenant Colonel Roger Kobelski with their request for help from the Federal Bureau of Investigation. He managed to make the arrangement for them to meet an agent, and it had been a complicated process.

The first hurdle had been Kobelski's counterpart, a prim young man in his mid-twenties by the name of Anthony Pendleton. Thus began a long series of cable-grams between Munich and Washington D.C. Kobelski was also called in to answer questions. It didn't take long before a load of paperwork built up that was gone over several times.

Then the bureaucratic fracas came to a sudden stop. The F.B.I. announced all was in order and ready to go. Pendleton was told to fetch the two Jewish guys and bring them in for a conference.

———

ROGER KOBELSKI, DAVID ARNSTEINER AND Yitzhak Cohen entered the F.B.I. building in Munich and were ushered down a long hallway to a door at the end. Their escort allowed them to enter and when they stepped inside Agent Anthony Pendleton was waiting for them.

"Sit down," Pendleton said rather briskly.

The trio did as ordered.

"Here is how it's going to work," Pendleton continued. "The F.B.I. is going to provide one hundred percent of the funding for the project."

Cohen shrugged. "That's fine with us."

"And one of you two Jewish gentlemen is going to Wichita, Kansas to carry on the investigation. Who will it be?"

Arnsteiner raised his hand. "That will be me."

"Excellent," Pendleton stated. "There is a troopship —the Queen Mary—that will be sailing to New York City. The vessel is returning American Armed Forces personnel to the States. You will share a stateroom with several officers. An F.B.I. Agent will meet you when the ship docks. He will go with you on a military flight to McConnell Air Force Base in Wichita. There you will be met by the chief agent there. His name is Steve Williams. He is going to arrange a partner for you to discover the answer to this puzzling situation. This individual will *not* be an F.B.I. agent. However, the man has done undercover work for the Bureau in the past."

"I see," Arnsteiner said, irritated by Pendleton's haughtiness. "Who will he be?

"A private detective by the name of Dwayne Wheeler."

CHAPTER 21

Two weeks after Roger Kobelski sent the photostats of the sketches to the Grenadier Guards Regiment, a communiqué from that unit was placed on his desk by Sergeant Carey "This just arrived, sir," the WAC informed him. "It was sent through British and American channels directly to you."

"Thank you, Sergeant," Kobelski responded. He wasted no time in opening the envelope and unfolding the missive inside to read.

From: Regimental Adjutant, Grenadier Guards

Re: Sketches for Identification

The two portraits you dispatched to this staff have been shown to the regimental headquarters, all battalion headquarters as well as the regimental officers and noncommissioned officers messes. Several similar identifications were made of the individual portrayed. All are the same with no other additional identifications.

The likeness is that of Nigel Hawthorne a former officer of this regiment. He was cashiered from the British Army due to embezzlement of funds. We have no knowledge of his present whereabouts.

Kobelski was thoughtful for a moment. It was obvious the disgraced officer was in Germany. Arnsteiner and Cohen had convinced him of that fact. If Hawthorne was in West Germany, the best place to find out more about him would be the Allied Criminal Investigation Division in the capital city of Bonn. He pressed the button on the intercom and Sergeant Carey immediately reappeared. "Yes, sir?"

"I need two things, Sergeant," Kobelski said. "I'll need a driver and sedan for a trip to Bonn first thing tomorrow morning as early as possible"

"I will make the arrangements as soon as I get back to my desk," Sergeant Carey said. She scribbled the information down in the notebook she always carried when called into Kobelski's office. "Anything else, sir?"

"Yes. I want you to send a message over the teletype to the Allied C.I.D. in that same city ASAP today. Classify it as urgent—I say again—*urgent* and make an afternoon appointment for me tomorrow with representatives from both the American and British sections. This is in regards to the location and activities of a suspect individual by the name of Nigel Hawthorne. Mention that he is a British subject and was cashiered from that nation's army."

She added that to her notes. "Will you need a confirmation?"

He nodded his head. "Good idea, Sergeant Carey."

The sergeant left to tend to her boss's orders.

———

THE NEXT DAY KOBELSKI WAS DRIVEN TO ALLIED C.I.D. headquarters in Bonn. His driver dropped him off at the front entrance to the building, then headed to the motor pool. He would remain at that location until summoned to pick up the colonel for the return drive to Sommerfeld.

Kobelski entered the lobby and presented his I.D. card to an M.P. guard. He was directed to a conference room on the second floor. The lieutenant colonel knocked on the indicated door and stepped inside. Two officers—an American captain and a British major—seated at a table stood up. Introductions with handshakes identified them as Captain Martin and Major Ross.

After all three were seated, Kobelski pulled the paperwork and photostats from his briefcase, giving each officer a copy. He waited while his companions perused the material.

Ross looked up. "I know this Hawthorne chap. At least I was present at his court-martial. That was...let me see...two or three years ago."

"I want to find out all I can about the man," Kobelski requested. "Can you begin with that trial?"

"Certainly," Ross said. "Gambling is what did him in. He had a long run of bad luck at an illegal Frankfurt casino. Someone from the gambling parlor reported his predicament to Soviet headquarters in the Russian Zone. The informer was obviously a Communist agent, since Hawthorne's difficulties were typical of what the Reds always look for when recruiting spies and moles. One of their operatives contacted Hawthorne and offered to settle his debts if he agreed to become an agent in their organization. If he refused, they would reveal his heavy gaming debts to British intelligence."

"That's what we Americans call being between a rock and a hard place," Kobelski remarked.

"Indeed!" Ross said. "He refused the offer, and being the mess officer for his regiment, he embezzled funds to cover his losses. He was found out, of course."

"I can imagine how that went over in the Grenadier Guards," Kobelski opined.

"He told them about the offer from the Reds in hopes his refusal to be a turncoat would earn him some leniency. That was a possibility, but when he was turned over to MI5 they wanted him to agree to become a double agent. Hawthorne, surprisingly, turned them down."

"Did he say why?" Kobelski asked.

"Hawthorne didn't like the idea of spying for anybody. However, from that moment on he was quite contrite and held nothing back about his gambling experience or the identification of the Soviet spy working in the casino. By doing this he hoped it would save him from disgracing his family if he were to be cashiered for conduct unbecoming an officer and gentleman. They weren't royalty or anything like that, but they were upper class and he had several male relatives holding responsible positions in the King's government. One of the Hawthornes had even been assigned to the British embassy in Washington throughout the war."

"How did that work out for him?"

"Not well," Major Ross replied. "Hawthorne said he would take the only honorable way out as a gentleman should."

"Suicide, right?" Kobelski asked.

"Absolutely," Ross replied. "He wrote a note revealing his misdeeds along with an apology. There was nothing to do after that, but fire a bullet into his head."

"God!" Kobelski exclaimed.

"But," Ross said, "in the end he didn't want to die. Consequently, he was cashiered in disgrace from the Grenadier Guards. He didn't dare return to England, so he stayed in Germany. The chap was cut off without a dime by his father, but he did find employment in the branch of a British bank in Frankfort. He should not have gotten the position under the circumstances, but he spoke fluent French and German and proved to be a valuable asset to his employers as long as he didn't handle any money."

Captain Martin spoke up. "Here's where I step in. As time passed, Hawthorne eventually became well acquainted with the financial dealings in postwar Europe. He came up with a scheme to participate in the Black Market. He formed a gang of American and British military personnel along with German gangsters. One of the Americans was a sergeant in the military police. The guy was young and not too wise. He spent his earnings lavishly to the point of having a beautiful mistress and a luxury apartment. Consequently, the sergeant was discovered and arrested. We grilled the hell out of the him, but he clammed up. A real tough guy. He ended up getting a discharge for the convenience of the government."

Kobelski's eyes opened wide. "Not a dishonorable discharge? Why the hell not?"

Martin shook his head. "I have no idea. I suspect it had something to do with public relations. The American command wanted to keep the incident undercover and hidden from the American public."

"What about Hawthorne?" Kobelski asked.

"We knew about the son of a bitch from undercover guys who informed us that he was making deals with other criminals. But we could never build a case against him. Presently he uses dozens of aliases and has paid off some very important people. He appears and disappears like some kind of phantom. "He gave Kobelski a hard look. "Now what can *you* tell *us* about him? And where did you get those sketches?"

At that point Kobelski had to fight down a desire to mention the missions of David Arnsteiner and Yitzhak Cohen. But he had given his word to the two men to allow them to work with the F.B.I., and he felt a strong obligation to the Zionists. The lieutenant colonel realized that his 35 percent Jewish side had compelled him to make that decision.

Kobelski cleared his throat and said, "I am not authorized to do that. Sorry."

———

HERBERT HOCK HAD FINISHED ANOTHER workweek as janitor at the *Wolflager* and rode into Sommerfeld on his bicycle. The youngster had a new document saved from the incinerator to turn over to the Displaced Persons Registration Office. He stopped by the group's headquarters and dropped it off, then continued on to his family's home for the weekend.

Pili the receptionist at the building wasted no time in taking the document to Yitzhak Cohen. He was at his worktable with David Arnsteiner planning the latter's activities upon his arrival in America. The pair were devising various methods for communications to use between them during the operation.

"Sorry to interrupt," Pili announced, laying down the information between the two men. "But it is another document from Herbert."

"Thank you," Cohen said. He unfolded the sheaf of papers and began reading. When he finished he gave

Arnsteiner a worried look. "It seems our antagonists have decided to not move any art out of America for the time being."

"I wonder what that can mean."

"It is very plain to me, my friend. It would appear that the number of paintings are so numerous they're clogging up the delivery system. So a break in operations is necessary. Bad luck that. And they also stopped all deliveries to Wichita, Kansas. At any rate, you carry on as originally planned. I will call a staff meeting to deal with this new development."

Chapter 22

I t was late morning when Dwayne parked at the curb
in front of Donna Sue's apartment house. He was in a
1936 Chevrolet Coupe borrowed from Elmer Pettibone
who owned the Roadhouse night club. Elmer was a
former bootlegger who used Dwayne to help with his
whiskey smuggling business.

The shamus noticed the absence of cars parked in the
neighborhood at that time of day. That was to his advantage since it meant there wouldn't be many people out on
the neighborhood street. He got out of the coupe wearing
a disguise that made him appear to be a repairman of
sorts. He was clad in overalls and wore a faded khaki baseball cap while carrying a tool box.

Dwayne went boldly into the building and up the
stairs to the third floor to Donna Sue's door. He took a
careful look around, donned a pair of gloves then took a
jimmy out of the box. In less than a minute he had pried
the door open and entered the apartment. He immediately pulled out a few drawers and threw the contents
around to leave an impression that a real burglar had

broken into the place. With that done, he grabbed her jewelry box.

His egress from the building was just as clandestine as the ingress, and he drove away totally unseen.

———

After further discussion regarding plans for the future, Dwayne and Donna Sue decided it was time for a Saturday work session in his office. They purchased a card table and a folding chair for her to use as a desk. The reason for the weekend task was that they had already laundered a couple of thousand dollars from Dwayne's hiding place in his apartment closet into the bank checking account. It was now time to prepare for future deposits. It had already been decided that most of the 400 dollars he received from Pete every two weeks would be designated as payments from both actual and nonexistent clients. And, of course, Dwayne still had yet to go to a fence to dispose of Donna Sue's gift jewels given her by Brian Murchison.

In order to facilitate concealing business dealings, Donna Sue had some invoice forms printed up with the words **WHEELER DETECTIVE AGENCY** across the top. There was a place below the firm name for listing clients' names, addresses and phone numbers.

"From now on use these invoices," she told Dwayne. "No matter if you're listing payments from real cases or made up ones, you must record the personal information by simply writing 'confidential' in the proper spaces."

"Gotcha, toots."

She frowned. "I wish you'd stop saying that. It's rather annoying and I am *not* a 'toots'."

"Yes, ma'am."

"The rest of the form is used to describe the actions you took on the cases."

He grinned and winked. "I wish you'd stop saying 'cases'. I don't have 'cases,' I have 'capers'."

"As you wish, Sam Spade."

Donna Sue had worked out a formula for the number of capers to coincide with the amount of money being laundered. She pulled out a dozen invoice forms from the box and laid them on his desk. "These are the first dummy documents. Have a seat and start listing the sham capers and phony customers. Describe various activities you would have done if these were genuine. And list the phony customers by numbers. So let your creative writing skills run wild, Shakespeare."

"Gotcha—er, yes, ma'am."

It turned out he liked that part of the swindle best. He sat down and began making up dates and times followed by activities such as surveillance, tailing suspects, questioning witnesses, divorces, debt collecting, etc.

Donna Sue went back to her work of scheduling payments and deposits to be made in the Kansas Merchant and Farmers Bank. She had to keep the I.R.S. in the back of her mind and concentrate on avoiding glaring errors or obvious exaggerations in the financial proceedings.

A half hour passed and she looked over at Dwayne. He was completely enthralled as he scribbled away on the forms. Donna Sue thought he looked like he was having too much fun. She got up and walked over to his desk. "How are you doing?"

"Great! I'm describing the phony capers like you told me to."

She picked up several of the forms and looked at them for an instant, then exclaimed, "You practically have crime novels here! Going down dark alleys! Shooting it out with bad guys! Fist fights! Mysterious people hiding in the shadows! Even gun molls!"

He grinned proudly. "Pretty good, huh?"

"What we need," Donna Sue said trying to be as calm as possible, "is something dull and routine. Something easily forgotten. Something that is normal. Something that the I.R.S. will find unremarkable. Something that would make them yawn."

"Hey! I've had some pretty dangerous times that I experienced for real! I solved a couple of murders, remember?"

"I know, Dwayne, and you already have backup for all that in the files in case somebody gets curious about them. Even newspaper clippings. Please do the phony ones over, sweetie."

Dwayne wadded up his literary masterpieces and tossed them into the wastebasket.

———

IT WAS MID-WEEK WHEN DWAYNE RECEIVED A late night call from Pete Van Dyke in New York City. The ringing phone woke him up. He sleepily responded, "Hullo."

"Dwayne, it's me, Pete. I have some important information for you."

Now Dwayne came wide awake, hoping it wasn't bad news. "What's going on?"

"There's been a change with the cabal. There'll be no mailings of tubes for awhile. And you are to destroy all mailing labels. Every single one, get it?"

"Jesus, Pete! Those have prepaid postage."

"It doesn't matter."

"Any particular reason for all this or is it none of my business."

"I have no explanation either, but evidently the art collectors are readjusting their arrangement. But not to worry, pal, this isn't the end of the operation. You'll still get your salary. Look at it this way; things will be easier for you."

Dwayne chuckled. "I'm not exactly weighed down now, Pete."

"That's true, I guess. So how many tubes do you have in the strongbox?"

"A dozen or so I guess."

"Well, that's probably anywhere between five to ten paintings in each tube," Pete surmised. "So I'm sure things will start rolling again before long. At least I hope so."

"As long as I get my salary, I don't give a shit," Dwayne stated.

Pete laughed and hung up.

CHAPTER 23

Lieutenant Colonel Roger Kobelski contacted several intelligence and crime agencies in West Germany to garner as much information on Nigel Hawthorne as possible. Unfortunately, the number of responses from those organizations was discouraging. The man may have been an upper-class Brit and a former officer in one of the Kingdom's most prestigious and elite regiments, but the wily son of a bitch was a born criminal mastermind. The problem was that he had made no careless slips in his nefarious career. No matter how the authorities delved into accusations against him, they were unable to discover any solid evidence of the man's involvement.

"Damn!" Kobelski exclaimed aloud to himself. "The guy's worse than Moriarty!" He was referring to Professor James Moriarty, the problematic gentleman who was the worst and deadliest antagonist that Sherlock Holmes faced in Sir Arthur Conan Doyle's crime stories.

Kobelski turned to his intercom. "Sergeant Carey, put in a call to Yitzhak Cohen, please. Tell him I would like to meet with him and Mister Arnsteiner here in my office at their earliest convenience. Mention it involves Nigel Hawthorne."

———

A FEW HOURS LATER DAVID ARNSTEINER WITH Yitzhak Cohen sitting beside him, drove his small Citroën sedan up to the gate of the visitors parking lot at American Sector Headquarters. They presented their special I.D.s to the M.P. guard and were waved inside.

After parking, the two Jews hurried through various manned check points in the building until reaching Kobelski's office. Sergeant Carey announced them on the intercom and the two hurried inside, anxious to hear what information the colonel had on Nigel Hawthorne.

Kobelski had arranged two chairs in front of his desk for the session. Arnsteiner and Cohen settled down on the furniture, and gave the American officer their undivided attention.

"Well," the lieutenant colonel began. "I made a call to the Allied Criminal Investigation Division to find out about the very illusive Mister Hawthorne. It was amazing to learn that this highborn English gentleman has apparently warped into a first rate criminal genius. He went from a respectable and commendable officer in the Grenadier Guards into what we Americans would call a racketeer gang boss. I can confidently say that he is worse than Al Capone."

"Mmm," Arnsteiner mused. "How many times as he been arrested?"

"None—I say again—*none!*"

"I see," Cohen remarked. "Then how many times has he been detained by the authorities then released?"

"The answer is the same."

Arnsteiner leaned forward. "Do you mean to say that Hawthorne is a known criminal mastermind, yet has never been detained? Arrested? Or even a suspect?"

"Oh, he's been a suspect a good number of times," Kobelski replied. "The authorities—both military and civil—are aware of his clandestine activities outside the law, but not one shred of solid evidence has ever been collected against the man. And no credible witnesses have been found that could or would testify against him. No concrete proof until now."

This was like giving Arnsteiner and Cohen an injection of adrenalin.

Kobelski continued. "He can easily be charged with fraud for his claim to be Major Hawkins. We have his I.D. photos, the sketches made from them, and it will only be a matter of time to gather testimony from various British officers of the Grenadier Guards regarding his identity and the circumstances of his being cashiered for embezzlement."

Arnsteiner and Cohen exchanged glances, then Cohen stated, "We do not want you to have him arrested, Roger."

Kobelski frowned. "What the hell do you mean by that?"

"He belongs to us," Arnsteiner stated in a firm tone of voice. "We do not want you to take him into custody. We plan to assassinate him as quickly as feasible."

Kobelski glared back at him. "Don't hand me that bullshit! You have no authority to demand we give you complete access to him."

Cohen argued, "We have a moral obligation as Jews to take his life. He is now working with an illegal quasi-military organization that committed genocide against our people."

Kobelski shrugged. "Then how in hell do you expect to deal with him?"

"I will say no more than we will develop the means of locating and trapping the man," Arnsteiner continued.

Kobelski was suddenly suspicious. "You know where that son of a bitch is, don't you?"

Arnsteiner ignored the question. "We have a bit of time before we can commit extreme prejudice on his person. If you capture him, our principle Nazi enemies will know you will get valuable information about their organization. However, if he is killed, they will know there is no danger of them being exposed. They will resume their normal operations and eventually we'll move in on them."

"You sound pretty sure of yourselves," Kobelski grumbled.

"Roger, we are most certainly sure of ourselves," Arnsteiner said.

"This case is a serious responsibility for me," Kobelski protested. "The Allied C.I.D. could wring a lot of information out of him. It could cut down crime in West Germany and other places in the civilized world by a hell of a lot. The authorities would hang me out to dry if I agreed to let you croak Hawthorne instead of bringing him in for trial."

Arnsteiner spoke thoughtfully and carefully. "You may not be a hundred percent Jewish, Roger, but much of your ancestry includes our people. We in the *Tsad'yod-mem* are avengers. Surely some of your distant kin died in the camps. And there is no doubt that much of the property that is now in the hands of the neo-Nazis once belonged to people whose blood flows through your veins."

"That's right," Cohen said. "And who will know you

are aware of the killing? In fact, neither I nor David will be linked in any fashion to the deed."

Roger Kobelski fell into a silence of several long moments. He had seen two of the death camps with the dead stacked naked in piles when his intelligence unit advanced into Germany during the war. He had looked into the vacant eyes of the starving survivors. Even Hawthorne's felonies did not come close to the heinous crime of attempting to wipe out an entire race. It could be that a few or perhaps many of those men and women had blood connections to his family. He cleared his throat.

"Kill the son of a bitch."

"May I remind you that it may be some time before that happens?"

Roger sighed. "Whatever!"

———

WHEN DONNA SUE CAME HOME ON THE EVENING that her place was "burglarized," she immediately called the Wichita Police Department. The usual investigation and interviews followed as they examined the apartment. The burglary detail figured it was someone she knew since the thief was aware of the jewelry. She pointed out the guy had pulled out drawers and thrown things around in searching for loot. The discovery of the valuables was luck on his part. She also mentioned there had been other burglaries in the building over the years.

The police concluded their investigation by dusting for fingerprints. With all that done the manager installed a new lock on the door.

———

David Arnsteiner and Yitzhak Cohen did not return to the *Tsad'yod-mem* office after leaving Lieutenant Colonel Roger Kobelski. Instead, Arnsteiner drove his Citroën straight to a rundown neighborhood on the south side of Sommerfeld. He pulled up at a curb beside a public telephone. Cohen got out and went to the instrument. He fed in a coin, then spoke for less than a minute before returning to the car.

"Mordecai says he'll meet us at an outside table by that tavern on *Ahorne Strasse*," Cohen said.

Arnsteiner went up the street and made a U-turn to go back a couple of blocks. When he reached *Ahorne Strasse*, he went past their destination half a block and parked. They walked up the street to where a half dozen tables were set outside a tavern. The only drinkers were a couple enjoying each other's company as well as the beer on the far side.

A waiter appeared and Cohen ordered three steins of brew stating they were waiting for a friend to join them. A few moments later a small man with rounded shoulders and a meek appearance joined them. The bespectacled individual was Mordecai Hod. He greeted the two men in Yiddish. "*Gut morg'n.*"

Cohen replied in Hebrew, "*Bokehr tov.*"

Arnsteiner chuckled. "Good morning. That translates both greetings into English."

Cohen was serious when he said, "Mordecai, you must learn Hebrew. The Yiddish language will not be allowed in the Jewish State. It is too much like German."

"My wife Ester is helping me to do exactly that," Mordecai assured him

At about that time the beer was served and the three men began speaking in low tones. Cohen asked, "Do you have any reports on Nigel Hawthorne?"

"He has been away for several weeks but is back now," Mordecai replied. He was the concierge in the building where Hawthorne lived with his mistress. "I am sure you remember he is calling himself Jones."

"Of course," Arnsteiner acknowledged.

Mordecai continued. "I have not been able to find out where he went since his return to the Üppig Nachbarshaft neighborhood of Munich. I tried different subtle questions and statements to get him to converse with me, but he never answers. Nor does his mistress. However, my wife has been able to speak to the woman briefly now and then."

Arnsteiner was worried. "Remember that we do not want Ester to know too much about our activities."

Mordecai took a thoughtful sip of beer. "Ester is aware we are involved in a Zionist cause and understands she cannot be told too much. However, she will help us as much as she can."

"We appreciate the devotion she is showing us," Yitzhak assured him.

Mordecai finished his beer and stood up. "*Luhitraot*," he said, then winked and added. "How's that in Hebrew?"

"An excellent goodbye, Mordecai," Arnsteiner said.

He and Cohen watched the thin little man walk down the street, looking more like a bank clerk than a Zionist secret agent.

CHAPTER 24

D wayne and Donna Sue's plans for the Wheeler
Detective Agency ripened to the point where they
were able to lease office space on the second floor of the
Wheeler Kelly Hagny Building; A.K.A. the WKH Building. The location was under the local F.B.I.'s office on the
third floor where Dwayne's fellow crime-fighter Agent
Steve Williams was headquartered. Donna Sue had left her
job at Dawson Construction two weeks previously and
taken the position of office manager of the new business.

The office was rather small compared to some of the
others in the building, but all the metal chairs, desks and
file cabinets were brand new and up-to-date in the late
1940s style. Also Dwayne and Donna Sue each had a new
Remington typewriter.

A small reception area was located at the entrance,
where Donna Sue's desk was located. Besides administrative tasks, her other duties were to answer the phone and
screen callers who wished to speak to the shamus. The
door to Dwayne's office was located behind her position.

This was where Dwayne would confer with potential customers.

The agency had a rather uncomplicated and inexpensive intercom system that was a direct wire from Donna Sue's desk that went along the floor and up to the ceiling, then through a hole into Dwayne's domain. The connection continued to the instrument on his desk. In actuality they could easily converse by speaking loudly to each other through the walls, but Donna Sue thought it would give an appearance of an up-to-date and efficient investigative organization if it had electronic communication.

The final task in this preliminary activity was to place small but permanent classified advertisements in both the *Wichita Eagle* and *Wichita Beacon* newspapers describing the services offered. Donna Sue also made arrangements to have an ad scheduled for the next edition of the Bell Telephone Company's yellow pages. The last thing done was making a call to the Reliable Answering Service to give them the new phone number.

Donna Sue's first duty of the day was to check in with the answering service to see if there were any phone messages for the Wheeler Detective Agency. Unfortunately, business was not particularly brisk except for the pseudo capers that Dwayne invented so they could funnel funds from his closet into the deposits in the Kansas Merchant and Farmers Bank. Payments on the loan were made through the money orders that Pete Van Dyke sent regularly every four weeks.

Bored but optimistic, the couple settled in with high hopes.

———

IT WAS THREE O'CLOCK IN THE MORNING AND the posh Üppig Nachbarshaft neighborhood in Munich was quiet in the predawn darkness. A taxi pulled up in front of a luxurious apartment building. Despite the size of the edifice and the wealth of its residents, it bore no name. Nor was there a directory in the lobby. Blanket anonymity was what attracted the residents to rent the expensive accommodations at that preferred location.

After the cab stopped, it was easy to discern that the two passengers were very special since the driver got out and opened the door for them. It was also apparent that the man and woman, in expensive evening dress, were more than a little intoxicated. The male handed the cabbie a handful of bills.

"*Behalten Sie den Rest!*" he said, telling the driver to keep the change.

"*Danke sehr,*" the cabbie replied gratefully, then got back into the vehicle and drove off.

The man put his arm around the woman in a drunken manner and they walked unsteadily toward the entrance to the building's lobby. Mordecai Hod, sitting at the concierge station inside quickly got to his feet and opened the door.

"*Guten Morgan, Herr und Frau* Jones," Mordecai greeted the couple in English and German. "Did you have an enjoyable evening at the clubs?"

"We certainly did, Mordecai," Nigel Hawthorne replied with a laugh. "Tell me, don't you ever sleep?"

"I nap when I am able," Mordecai said, surprised at the man's friendliness. "A concierge must be on duty practically 24 hours a day. And anyway, I have my wife Ester to help me."

"Oh!" Lale Altner, Hawthorne's German mistress,

exclaimed. "You and Ester work way too much. Perhaps you should hire some help."

Mordecai, noting the foolishness of her statement, shook his head. "We like our job and the residents too much to want to share you with anyone else."

"You are both sweet," Lale said. She turned to Hawthorne. "Aren't they, *Liebling*?"

"Aren't they what?"

"Sweet! Aren't they sweet?"

"Who?"

"*Mein Gott!*" Lale exclaimed. "Never mind!"

"Let's go," Hawthorne said drunkenly. "Or you'll start working here at the concierge desk yourself."

Now laughing, the couple headed for the elevator as Ester Hod stepped out into the lobby from the apartment just behind the station. She wore a quilted robe and had curlers in her hair.

"Mordecai," she said. "Hurry and write down the time of their return in your log."

"I did that as soon as the taxi pulled up."

Ester sighed. "I wish the *Tsad'yod-mem* did not require so much information. Most of it seems useless and a waste of time."

"It is all for a good cause," Mordecai said. "Come on. Let us go inside to our own bed. If anyone needs us they can ring the bell."

Hawthorne and Lale reached the elevators. But instead of taking one of the automatic conveyances, they continued past them to a door that led to the alley. The couple, now appearing cold sober, stepped out and immediately got into the backseat of a car that was waiting for them.

A chauffeur and Police Commissioner Werner Ullman

were in the front. The driver stepped on the accelerator and headed down the alley to the street.

———

THE MORNING RUSH HOUR IN DOWNTOWN Wichita was just beginning to taper off as Dwayne Wheeler and Donna Sue Connors entered the WKH Building. The couple walked up the stairs to the second floor, stepping out of the stairwell into the hallway. They continued down to the door where the words **WHEELER DETECTIVE AGENCY** were lettered neatly on the frosted glass window of the portal.

Dwayne went into his office while Donna Sue took off her hat and put her purse in the desk drawer. She sat down and dialed the Reliable Answering Service. "Hi, Millie," she said after their point of contact responded. "This is Donna Sue. Any calls for us?"

"You got one this morning, hon," Millie replied. "Kessler Bail Bonds wants you to give 'em a jingle."

Donna Sue thanked her, then hung up, speaking loudly to Dwayne. "You have a call from A.J."

Dwayne quickly dialed A.J. Kessler's number. The bondsman was agitated as he answered, "Izzat you, Dwayne?"

"Yep. What's up?"

"I got a bail jumper located and am gonna need some help taking him into custody. It's Freddy Baldwin."

"Oh, shit!"

"Yeah," A.J. said. "He's charged with armed robbery and his lawyer Andy Fawcett was actually able to get the judge to grant him bail. I figgered the judge knew what he was doing, so I didn't mind bailing Freddy out. And, of course, the son of a bitch didn't show up for his court date. Are you inter'sted in giving me a hand bringing him in?"

"Sure. I'll drive right over."

Dwayne grabbed his hat and went through the door, speaking quickly to Donna Sue. "A.J. needs me to help take a runner into custody."

She started to say something about that not being a good idea, but Dwayne was through the door and on his way.

———

A.J. Kessler, bail bondsman, was a well-groomed and most fastidious dresser with thick black hair and a handlebar moustache that curled up on the ends. He was also a little person, standing about four and a half feet tall. He owned a 1941 Packard that was specially-built and designed to accommodate his physical requirements. By using a couple of sofa pillows on the seat, along with built-up accelerator, clutch and brake pedals A.J. was able to drive safely and efficiently. He used a walking stick to reach the starter on the floorboard.

Another unusual feature of the vehicle was the lack of handles on the inside of the rear doors. This arrangement had been installed to prevent passengers from being able to get out of the car by themselves. Most of these individuals in the backseat were not voluntary riders. They were, in fact, prisoners of the diminutive bondsman. A.J. Kessler went after jumpers with a vengeance. And when he caught one, he took them to the county jail in that atypical Packard as they sat fuming helplessly in the back.

A.J.'s personal firearm was a Beretta Model 1922 nine-millimeter semi-automatic pistol. This compact weapon fit A.J.'s small hand quite well. Additionally, he had a self-designed telescoping baton made of stainless steel. Its one-foot length could be doubled by the quick flick of a spring-loaded release button. The little man practiced constantly with the device, and could wield it fast and effectively against larger opponents. His attacks left large red welts even through thick clothing.

———

A.J. KESSLER BAIL BONDS WAS A CEMENT BLOCK building down on Main Street a little south of the police station and jail. Dwayne drove around to the rear and parked beside A.J.'s Packard. He walked to the front door where the little man's secretary Jill Stuart kept her desk.

She gave Dwayne a dirty look as always. He had dated her a couple of times in the past but broke off the relationship because she lived with her parents. The girl's father objected to having his daughter go out with a gumshoe. Jill recognized that Dwayne was turned off by the aggravation so she suggested they elope. But the shamus nixed the idea vehemently. At that time, he had only recently lost Donna Sue to Brian Murchison and was still hurting from the breakup. Besides the last thing he wanted to do was marry a young girl just out of high school who didn't even have her own apartment.

Now, still glowering at him, Jill grumbled, "A.J. is waiting for you in his office."

"Thank you, Miss Stuart."

"Up yours, Mister Wheeler."

Dwayne rapped on the door and stepped inside. "What've we got going?" he asked, sitting down.

A.J. took a deep breath. "Under normal conditions this would be a piece of cake. But you know Freddy Baldwin as well as I do. What we got to deal with is six-foot-four-inch, two hunnerd pounds of romping, stomping craziness. I don't have to remind you that Freddy is as mean as he is stupid, which puts him in the category of a male silverback gorilla with an impacted tooth."

"Mmm," Dwayne mused. "Why don't we just use our gats on the son of a bitch if he fights us? I don't mean killing him. Just shoot him in the knees."

"It might happen," A.J. conceded.

"I'm gonna be ready for anything," Dwayne said. "So what's the full picture here?"

"The bond is for twenty-five thousand bucks," A.J. said. "And I put down ten percent as usual which was twenty-five hunnerd bucks. As you know I can't get that refunded from the court. It has to come from my customer."

"Wait a minute," Dwayne said. "How the hell did that dickhead come up with enough collateral to cover the cost?"

"His brother-in-law Willard Newly owns a machine shop that does special work for Boeing. His wife Clara, who is Freddy's sister, works in the plant as the book-keeper. They make big bucks."

"Okay. I understand. So what's on our agenda?"

"Freddy is hiding at the Newly home in north Wichita. Willard is scared shitless of his brother-in-law and wants him to get out of his life. Unfortunately, Freddy's sister Clara doesn't want her brother taken to jail since it's obvious he's gonna be doing a long stretch up at Lansing. He's been in prison four or five times and has always served the full sentences by being less than a model prisoner."

Dwayne shrugged. "You got any idea how we're gonna get into the house without breaking and entering."

"That ain't gonna be a problem," A.J. said. "Newly has given me a key to the back door. He has talked his wife into going with him to spend a couple of days at his cousin's house up in Newton. She don't know about the help he's giving me to get her brother. Naturally Freddy is gonna stay at the house while they're gone. So we got to strike while the iron is hot."

"Which is today?"

"Not quite," A.J. replied. "I figger it'd be better if we waited until dark and snuck through the back door. We won't have to make any noise since we got that key. I'll pick you up at midnight and we'll go over there."

"I'll bring along my good ol' reliable brass knuckles, too."

A.J. wasn't sure that was a good idea. "Them things mess folks up too much."

"Okay," Dwayne said. "I got a pair without protrusions on 'em. It's a smooth metal model. One good straight punch in the nose will break it and blacken both eyes so the guy can't see. No fractured facial bones."

A.J. nodded his approval. "See you at midnight, ol' buddy."

CHAPTER 25

Donna Sue renewed her protests when she saw Dwayne put on his shoulder holster and slip a pair of brass knuckles into his pants pocket. She was sleeping over in his apartment because of his midnight departure to go with A.J. Kessler. Dwayne had described the fugitive they were after and she didn't like the idea of his helping the little man bring in a snarling, defiant giant of a brute who was vicious and merciless.

She displayed one of her ferocious frowns, hissing, "Are you out of your mind? Do you want to get beat up bad? Or worse? A.J. is a nice guy but he's also a *little* nice guy!"

"Listen, sweetie. I'm packing my pistol in case things do get out of hand."

Her tirade continued unabated to the point Dwayne sensed she was truly fearful of what might happen. But Donna Sue had never seen the bondsman in action with his extendable baton. Little or not, A.J. could be hell on earth for an opponent of any size. Besides Dwayne had already agreed to help him and it would have been both unfair and unmanly to back out. But Donna Sue was absolutely correct about describing Freddy Baldwin as a "snarling, defiant giant of a brute."

This bail jumper was a thug with pale blue eyes and straw blond hair. He wore the stringy locks long and was generally a week to a month behind in shaving; not to mention bathing. He was considered the poster boy for sadistic brutality to those who knew him. He was insensitive to pain and had been known to allow lesser challengers to hit him a number of times before he reacted. This always resulted in beating and stomping his adversaries into bleeding, bruised hunks of human flesh with serious fractures of skull and/or limbs.

Baldwin's sixth grade male teacher—when the hulk was fifteen years old—had a physical altercation with the boy in a classroom. The man managed to subdue the kid but ended up with painful injuries. Afterward, he described Freddy Baldwin as being a combination of Neanderthal and rabid pit bulldog.

Now back in his apartment, sitting with Donna Sue, Dwayne Wheeler noted it was a quarter to midnight. He got his hat, pistol and brass knuckles along with an extra set of handcuffs. The fugitive was so large that it might be necessary for two sets of the restraints to cuff his hands behind his back.

Dwayne headed for the door with Donna Sue following, going down to the street to wait for A.J. The couple stood under a tree by the curb where Donna Sue had parked the Buick. Dwayne tried some light conversation, but her reaction was one of utter silence punctuated by angry glares. He was glad when he saw A.J. drive down the street and brake to a stop in front of them.

The little man noted Donna Sue. "Hey there, lady!" he called out cheerfully.

"Hello, A.J.," she replied in a sullen voice.

"See you later, sweetie pie," Dwayne said, giving her a kiss on the lips. Then he quickly joined the bondsman in his special automobile.

———

DWAYNE AND A.J. DIDN'T TALK MUCH DURING the ride to their destination. Both had been in that neighborhood a few times and knew they would be entering a fairly well-to-do locality.

By the time they arrived at the house both were mentally prepared for what faced them. A.J. parked and turned off the ignition, sitting in silence for a moment. "Ready?"

"Willing and able," Dwayne replied.

It was a dark cloudy night and Dwayne noted they would have to go through a gate to get to the back door. "I hope there ain't a dog."

"Newly told me they would take the pooch with 'em on their visit," A.J. replied. "Anyhow he said it was one of them little fuzzy lapdogs. The critter belongs more to Clara than Willard." He stopped and surveyed the front of the house.

It had a large picture window and Dwayne remarked, "I hope we don't get thrown through that thing."

"No kidding!" A.J. agreed. "Okay. We'll go around to the back door, then across the kitchen and to the first door on the left. That's where Freddy will be sleeping."

"We *hope* he'll be sleeping," Dwayne stated.

"Yeah," A.J. said. "We do hope that." They walked through the gate to the rear of the house. A.J. pointed to a window. "That's where he is. Look in and check to see if we'll be able to see anything."

Dwayne put his face close to the screen. "It's dark as hell in there, A.J. We're gonna have to turn on a light to jump him."

"We'll just have to do our best."

They continued to some steps leading up to the back door. A.J. pulled out a key and quietly inserted it into the lock. There was a click and the door opened. The little man grinned. "I was kind of hoping it wouldn't work."

Dwayne grinned back. "Me, too."

A.J. led the way into the kitchen. A street light in front of the house cast a dull glow over the living room. The little man nodded toward an interior entrance indicating it was the target area. They eased their way down a short hallway and noted the door was open. By then their eyes were used to the semi-darkness and both caught sight of a very large man in nothing but shorts, stretched out the bed fast asleep.

"Okay," Dwayne whispered. "You turn on the light and I'll lead the way."

A.J. felt for a light switch, then took his baton and pressed the release button to expand the length. He nudged the switch and a bright light burst out over the bedroom. Dwayne, noting Baldwin was face down, leaped on the man, straddling his legs. At the same time, he pulled a set of handcuffs from his jacket pocket.

"Aaargh!" bellowed Baldwin as he quickly got to his hands and knees. Dwayne hit the man as hard as he could on the back of the neck with a closed fist.

"Aaargh!" Baldwin straightened up with such quickness that Dwayne was thrown off him, ending up on the floor.

A.J. charged with his baton and gave an overhand swing that hit the fugitive from shoulder to chest, leaving an ugly red welt.

"Aaargh!" Baldwin roared for the third time as he turned from Dwayne and grabbed A.J., throwing him against the far wall. The little guy bounced off and ended up flat on his face.

Dwayne had slipped his right hand into his brass knuckles, using it to strike his quarry one more time in the back of the neck.

"Aaargh!" Baldwin spun around and delivered a powerful left cross that connected with Dwayne's jaw, sending the shamus staggering sideways to collide with a chest of drawers. The impact sent a shockwave from his right shoulder to wrist that quickly evolved into numbness.

Now A.J. was on his feet facing Baldwin's back and he swung the baton. This time it left a diagonal weal from the man's shoulder to his buttocks. The wallop had drawn blood that spattered back on the little bondsman.

"Aaargh!" Baldwin yelled as he turned to face the attacker.

A.J. was ready. He made a quick looping movement with his hand, swinging the baton down and up to connect directly with Baldwin's scrotum.

"Ooow!"

The big man collapsed to the floor, his hands on his damaged testes.

The bondsman knew the fight was over. Dwayne, limping, looked down at the moaning bond jumper. He spoke with a noticeable tone of relief in his voice. "I guess all we got left to do is cuff the son of a bitch."

"I got a hog-tie harness in the trunk of my car," A.J. informed him. "It'll make it easier to tote him out of here. I'll be right back."

Dwayne drew his .45 semi-auto from the shoulder holster and pulled the slide back to chamber a round. He aimed the weapon directly down at Baldwin, speaking with growing discomfort as his jaw began to swell. "You as much as blink—and I'm gonna—blow your fucking—head off. Understand?"

"Uh huh...uh."

Chapter 26

The British Cunard Line's great ocean liner the *Queen Mary* was a prestigious vessel that was launched in 1934 to operate between Great Britain and the United States. She transported her passengers in luxurious surroundings with excellent cuisines from several galleys. Concerts, dances, games and gymnasiums were also available for the pleasure of the travelers. Even the lower class voyagers enjoyed a comfortable atmosphere as they rode the waves across the great North Atlantic Ocean.

However, at the outbreak of World War II this great lady did her bit in the fight against Nazi Germany. She shed her china dishware, silverware, carpets, artwork, etc. to participate in the conflict as a troop carrier. She and her sister ship the *Queen Elizabeth* could each carry 15,000 soldiers on the North Atlantic convoy routes without danger from German U-Boats. The two vessels' speed and maneuverability made it impossible for even the best German submarine commanders to launch torpedoes accurately enough to score hits.

After the final victory of World War II the two ships stayed in service to bring home American soldiers for their return to civilian life. Now tied up in the New York Harbor, the *Queen Mary* had just completed a run with returnees. The unloading of these soon-to-be civilians was completed within a couple of hours after docking.

However, a special passenger was still on board, quartered in a cabin among those of the ship's officers. He was treated as a very special traveler and shared the meals and relaxation of the wardroom. The vessel's rankers were much better off in that part of the ship than the enlisted men who were crammed below deck.

Before leaving port the ship's captain had briefed his staff on their unusual companion, explaining he was classified as a V.I.P. on a special mission. The officers found him affable and courteous, but not inclined to talk much. When the man did engage in conversation, he spoke with a German accent that had a dash of the British military style in it. Another curious aspect of the mysterious traveler was his cheap suit of clothes and a single leather suitcase that appeared to have been run over by a Mack truck. It was puzzling how someone so special would look like he belonged down with the enlisted soldiers.

This was David Arnsteiner who was to be met by an F.B.I. agent charged with arranging his trip to Wichita, Kansas. Once there he would be put in touch with a private detective under Bureau supervision to locate works of stolen art thought to be hidden in that mid-American city.

Arnsteiner had brought some reading material with him. It amounted to three novels by Charles Dickens, i.e. *Great Expectations, Nicholas Nickleby* and *Bleak House.* When he was serving with the Jewish Brigade, his knowledge of English had improved to such a degree that his

British commanding officer introduced him to the author he considered the best in the English language. Arnsteiner, armed with an English-German dictionary, began reading the novels while growing more fluent with each perusal.

———

NOW ARNSTEINER SAT ALONE IN THE OFFICERS' ward room and had just finished Chapter XLI in *Nicholas Nickleby* where Mrs. Nickleby was getting romantic with a neighbor gentleman. He was interrupted when the ship's captain and a civilian appeared. The captain nodded toward Arnsteiner. "This is our special passenger you've inquired about."

The civilian thanked the captain then looked at the man. "David Arnsteiner?"

"Yes."

"I am Agent Lawrence Tomlinson, F.B.I.," he stated, showing an I.D. card. "You and I have a plane waiting for us."

Arnsteiner was glad his mission could begin. "Fine. I take it we shall be flying to the city of Wichita in Kansas."

Tomlinson shook his head. "That comes later. We'll be traveling to a government airfield in Virginia. Are you ready to leave?"

"Certainly," Arnsteiner replied. "All I have to do is put my toiletries in my suitcase." He quickly went to his cabin as Tomlinson waited.

———

BOTH DWAYNE WHEELER AND A.J. KESSLER WERE badly battered from their capture of the bail jumper

Freddy Baldwin. The shamus had a swollen jaw that had grown so painful it was difficult to understand him when he talked through swollen lips. This also meant he would be living on a diet of soup for several weeks. His right shoulder was also sore and bruised from bouncing off the chest of drawers.

As for A.J. Kessler, he had suffered a bump on his head from being thrown bodily against a wall. If it hadn't been for the little man making a lucky clout with his baton against Baldwin's testicles, the pair would have been in much worse shape. Possibly even dead.

But now the fugitive was locked down tight in the Saint Francis Hospital's confinement unit under the supervision of Sedgwick County. This meant that the money A.J. had put up for the bail was safe. He paid for both his and Dwayne's visit to the hospital's emergency room. Dwayne was worse off than A.J. since his right shoulder had to be replaced in its socket from being dislocated. That hurt even worse than when it was originally injured.

However, both could now relax and heal from their arrest mission. Almost.

Dwayne had to face yet another ordeal. And that was the wrath of Donna Sue Connors. When she'd gone to the hospital to pick up the shamus, his appearance shocked her into a frightened rage. Donna Sue even started to slap his face, but the sight of his bruised jaw stopped her. Instead she shrieked. "*I told you this whole bail bond thing was a stupid idea!*"

"Ba' luck," he said, trying to speak through his swollen lips.

"*What if that guy had a gun and shot you?*"

"Butee dint."

"Oh, God!" Donna Sue moaned. "You can't even speak clearly!"

They went out to the hospital parking lot and got into the Buick. Donna Sue settled behind the wheel, glancing at him with a fierce frown as she drove onto the street. "If things had gone wrong in that fiasco, what would happen to the business we're trying to build up? And what about the loan you took out? Don't forget you wouldn't be able to do your work for Pete Van Dyke! You wouldn't be able to do work for *anybody*!"

"But dint hoppen."

Donna Sue continued. "How could we pay the rent on the office? How could *I* pay the rent on *my* apartment? Remember I quit my job at Dawson Construction! I swear to God this is like you used to be! Are we going to have to deal with more stupid stuff on your part?"

"Notnee mor."

She calmed down a little after driving a few blocks. "I want you to promise me you won't do anything I don't want you to do. Remember you're a prestigious business man now. You have a reputation to worry about."

"Okee," Dwayne acknowledged.

"I'm not going to get pissed off over minor stuff, Dwayne, but if you ever, ever again put yourself in immediate danger I'm gonna shoot you dead! Understand?"

He nodded, grimacing at the pain in his jaw.

CHAPTER 27

David Arnsteiner and Agent Lawrence Tomlinson flew in a C-47 transport from a government airport outside of New York City to Langley Air Force Base, Virginia. Arnsteiner enjoyed getting a bird's eye view of the great nation he had always wanted to visit. What was most apparent to him was that the countryside showed no signs of war damage. The scene was pure tranquil beauty. Europe had many cities still not completely cleared away from the rubble of bomb and artillery damage.

The two men shared the aircraft with several large crates bearing the stenciled words **TOP SECRET** on all sides. Their arrival at the destination was at the same time the sunset was dipping out of sight on the western horizon.

THIS AIR BASE, DESTINED TO BE USED FOR MUCH of America's highly secret activities in the future, had been built in 1916 and named Langley Airfield. It was shared by the Army, Navy and the National Advisory Council for Aeronautics. During World War I it was used to train American aero squadrons for combat in Europe.

Later, the site saw the testing of air power modus operandi in the 1920s that included bombing missions on captured German warships in offshore exercises. This training and experimentation was performed along the United States' Atlantic coast. In 1946 the new Tactical Air Command was established on the station, and two years later the name was changed to Langley Air Force Base.

———

DAVID ARNSTEINER AND AGENT TOMLINSON stepped down the aluminum ladder from the C-47's fuselage, and walked across the tarmac toward the reception building. A jeep with a military police officer and a sergeant driver was just beyond the entrance. The officer nodded to Tomlinson. "Hello, Larry. It looks like you got here a tad early."

"I think we had a tailwind," Tomlinson said. He indicated his companion. "This is David Arnsteiner."

"How do you do," the officer said. "Passport please."

Arnsteiner, puzzled by the request, handed his over.

The officer compared the photograph with Arnsteiner's face. "Are you a German citizen?"

"Yes, but when the war started I was living and working on a communal farm in Palestine. I joined the Jewish Brigade of the British Army that was organized there. I served in the Middle East and Italy. Just a moment." He reached into his inside jacket pocket and pulled out a British I.D. card indicating prior military service.

The officer studied the small document before handing it back. "Well, you're obviously who you say you are. Hop in the jeep, fellahs. We'll drive you over to the SpecOps office."

Arnsteiner, sitting in the back of the jeep with Tomlinson, couldn't see much in the headlights as they traveled a couple of miles down a macadam road. The driver steered the vehicle onto a dirt roadway and continued to a gate with a guard shack. After the Jew was given another identity check by an MP NCO, they entered a compound and drove to the door of a nonde-script one-story frame building. It was painted olive drab and had no sign revealing its purpose.

The MP officer obviously knew the place as he climbed out of the jeep and led Arnsteiner and Tomlinson over to the front entrance. He opened the door and gestured for the pair to enter. They walked into a small room furnished only with wooden benches that were obviously there for visitors. The MP officer exited through a door leading deeper into the interior of the wooden structure.

Ten minutes passed and a rather physically impressive man stepped into the room. He was clad in an olive-drab windbreaker over khaki overalls and sported a western style hat pushed back on his head. A pair of badly worn military boots completed his ensemble. Arnsteiner noted the guy needed a shave on his craggy countenance.

The rugged guy nodded to Tomlinson. "How're you doing, Larry?"

"Okay."

The rugged guy looked at Arnsteiner. "You must be the Jew."

"I am Jewish, yes," Arnsteiner said, realizing he wasn't going to learn the man's name.

"I'm here to give you a briefing," the rugged guy said. "It's the same briefing that was given to your cohorts in Germany yesterday. We know what you're doing in that building in Sommerfeld, West Germany with the displaced persons sign on it. We know you're all members of the *Tsad'yod-mem*." His pronunciation of the Hebrew words was atrocious. "And we also know that among your activities is the killing of Nazi criminals."

Arnsteiner was annoyed by his attitude. "We are also recovering property of Jews who were sent off to the camps or fled Germany. That is the one reason I'm over here."

"I know why you're here," the rugged guy said irritably. "Your mission is cleared to begin and you'll get all the cooperation you need from us Yanks."

"I am glad to hear that."

"Now listen up and listen up good," the rugged guy growled. "That organization of yours is forbidden to assassinate, interrogate or arrest any Nazi criminals. All that sort of activity is the responsibility of the Allied governments. They also need some of them Krauts to aid in dealing with the Soviet Union. They have vital information on the Reds' tactics, customs, aims and other methodology they employ. The relationship between Stalin and the West is deteriorating to dangerous levels. Do you understand?"

"Yes."

"The Allies will punish those Nazi criminals that are useless to us," the rugged guy continued. "Therefore I have been authorized to warn you that any disobedience of those instructions will be severely dealt with."

"I understand."

The rugged guy relaxed a bit. "I am also authorized to tell you that the government of the United States approves of and will be supportive of establishing a Jewish state in Palestine." At that point the rugged guy actually winked and grinned at Arnsteiner. "When you guys are a sovereign nation, you'll be able do any goddamn thing you want with the Nazi bastards that have escaped our net." He looked at Tomlinson. "See you again sometime, Larry."

With that, the rugged man left the room. Tomlinson turned to Arnsteiner. "Well, are you ready for that trip to McConnell Air Force Base? It's located south of Wichita, Kansas. But it'll take a few days to arrange things. Don't worry, though, we'll have some comfortable quarters here and be able to eat in the officers' mess."

"I cannot argue with that," Arnsteiner replied, feeling both irritated and grateful toward the rugged guy.

———

LAWYER ANDY FAWCETT WAS ESCORTED BY A clerk through the Sedgwick County's district attorney department to the office of Deputy D.A. Bob Delaney. "Hello, Andy. I've been expecting you."

"I'm not surprised, Bob. My client Freddy Baldwin was viciously attacked by that fucking midget A.J. Kessler and the crazy gumshoe Dwayne Wheeler. The whole incident was an outrageous disregard of his Constitutional rights. He is still in Saint Francis Hospital recovering from serious injuries to his genitals that have affected his urinary system. To put it simple, Bob, the unfortunate man has been pissing blood. His kidneys are in bad shape. Bad shape indeed!"

"Uh huh," Delaney acknowledged.

Fawcett continued, "I know Freddy has a bad reputation and he's spent his time in prison for various crimes.

But he's quits with society on that lawlessness. And I am aware that he's now charged with armed robbery and I also concede that he missed a court date. But that does not give anyone the right to inflict grievous injury upon his person."

"What about the injuries he inflicted on Kessler and Wheeler?"

"Self-defense," Fawcett countered. "Therefore, I wish to lodge charges against those two guys."

Delaney shook his head. "Andy, I could try my damnedest but there's no way in hell I could prosecute a successful case against a legally certified bondsman and a licensed private investigator for injuring a felon like Freddy Baldwin."

Fawcett stood up. "Shit! That's what I figured you'd say, Andy. I'd like to remind you that bondsmen and private eyes don't rate high in public opinion." He sighed, "Well, there's always the civil court. See you later."

"You bet," Delaney said. "And there will also be a trial in criminal court when *I* prosecute Freddy Baldwin. I'll certainly be adding assault charges for attacking A.J. and Dwayne."

"*Touché*, ol' buddy," Fawcett said, heading for the door.

———

THE PHONE RANG ON DONNA SUE'S DESK AND she responded with a businesslike greeting. "Wheeler Detective Agency. Where may I direct your call?" When the caller answered the question, she raised her voice. "Dwayne. It's Pete Van Dyke."

Dwayne, in his office, picked up the phone and leaned back in his chair. "Hey, Pete. What's happening?"

"Just a small change in operations," Pete replied. "Things are shutting down completely for the time being. There's no telling how long this will be."

"I was wondering what was going on. There's no crisis looking us in the eye, is there?"

"No, not at all," Pete assured him. "There's always auctions and trades among our clientele. Maybe an argument between a couple of 'em popped up. Who can figure out the art world, huh? I just wanted to let you know in case you were starting to worry about the situation."

Dwayne started to tell him about his adventure with A.J. Kessler but quickly thought it might be unwise. Pete would be upset to find out he'd gotten a good pounding going after a bail jumper. "Well, thanks for letting me know, Pete. I'll be ready when business picks back up."

Donna Sue was standing in the door when Dwayne hung up. She gave him a look of curiosity. "What's going on?"

"Those art collectors aren't doing much right now. Pete said not to worry. Things will get back to normal."

She gave him a close look. "Your jaw is still swollen."

"Tell me about it. I'm so goddamn sick and tired of slurping soup I could puke."

"Serves you right," she opined, then went back to her desk in the small reception area.

CHAPTER 28

It was early evening when Attorney Andy Fawcett sat at the kitchen table in the home of Willard and Clara Newly, the brother-in-law and sister of Freddy Baldwin. They were not a handsome couple. Both were extremely overweight and had perpetual scowls on their faces. Willard sported a weird pattern of male hair loss that he tried to improve with a double comb-over. Clara had a noticeable moustache that came back thicker each time she shaved it off.

Right now she was irritated by her brother's treatment during his arrest by Dwayne and A.J. "I don't see why they don't throw those two bullies in jail for beating up Freddy. They're just as bad as gangsters."

Fawcett shrugged and assumed a sad, concerned expression on his face. "There's nothing we can do since the district attorney's office won't cooperate with us." Actually the lawyer was more than happy about the situation. Willard Newly owned a machine shop that made plenty of money from its association with Boeing Aircraft. He had a long term contract to manufacture airplane parts. That meant he was a well-healed client for Fawcett in defending Freddy in criminal court. And there was also another aspect to the case that would bring in even more money for the lawyer.

Fawcett cleared his throat. "Y'know, even if we can't press criminal charges against Kessler and Wheeler, we can sure as hell go after 'em in civil court."

"I don't understand," Willard said.

The lawyer grinned. "How about if we sue those two scalawags for about one hundred thousand dollars? And we don't have to convince an entire civil jury to win the case either. Only a majority of those good citizens would be enough to award a verdict of guilty."

Clara Newly declared, "Heavenly days!"

Her husband was also eager. "D'you think we could win that much money?"

"Sure," Fawcett assured him. "I've handled many such suits in my career right here in Wichita. I have a lot of experience handling cases like this one."

"My gosh!" Clara said. "We could sure use a hundred thousand dollars, couldn't we, Willard?"

He answered with a wide smile. "You bet! I could put in some more lathes and drill presses in the shop. That way I could get contracts from Beech Aircraft and Cessna as well as expanding my services to Boeing."

"Actually," Fawcett said, "you two'd get about sixty-six thousand seven hundred or so bucks. I get a third of the money. That'd be maybe thirty-three thousand three hundred and thirty dollars."

Clara displayed a ferocious grimace. "Why in heaven's name d'you get so much?"

Fawcett shrugged. "That's the way the law reads. In lawsuits we attorneys get a third of any successful settlements. After all, we have to look up facts, check the finer parts of the law regarding the case, file the suit and other complicated paperwork."

Willard looked at his wife. "Hell, woman, sixty-six thousand seven hundred dollars is nothing to sneeze at."

Clara started to protest, then hesitated and said, "Okay, Willard. I guess you're right. That's what we gotta do then."

Fawcett grinned. "I'll get started on filing the suit first thing tomorrow."

———

WHEN DWAYNE AND DONNA SUE WENT TO THEIR office a few mornings later, they settled in as usual without much to do. At least for Dwayne. Donna Sue had two items on her agenda, which were an appointment at a downtown beauty parlor that morning and checking in with the Reliable Answering Service. She tended to that latter task as soon as she sat down at her desk. She dialed the number and inquired if there were any messages. Millie, the young lady assigned to the Wheeler Detective Agency, gave an affirmative answer and indicated the F.B.I. wanted to speak with Dwayne as soon as possible.

Donna Sue hung up and called out, "Dwayne! Come out here!"

He appeared in the door. "What's going on?"

"Millie said that F.B.I. guy upstairs left a message for you. He wants to see you as soon as possible." She grimaced. "Have you been up to any shenanigans that I don't know about?"

Dwayne groaned, "No, hell no! How long are you gonna keep up that suspicious attitude of yours?"

"Until I'm certain you've settled down."

Dwayne, angry at her way of thinking, left the office

and walked to the stairwell. He ascended to the third floor then stepped out into the hallway, coming to a halt. Donna Sue's obvious distrust of him since the bail bond fiasco was starting to become more than just a little annoying. He went to a window and looked down at the activity on South Market Street, taking a couple of deep breaths to steady his mood.

It took a few moments, and when the shamus simmered down, he admitted to himself that he couldn't really fault Donna Sue for her attitude. As a youngster she had to quit school to help her mother support the family. Then, when grown, she had lost a good job at Boeing after the war because of her gender. That's not even considering Donna Sue had also experienced the worst of luck with the men in her life. That started with her father who had deserted them. Then there were two lousy husbands. The first had deserted her and the second ran away with a neighbor woman. Then Dwayne entered her life as an unreliable, happy-go-lucky boyfriend who didn't show much get-up-and-go except when he was on a caper. And those didn't pay very much money. Even when he did get a few bucks together he pissed it away betting on the ponies. When she broke up with him, she linked up with wealthy Brian Murchison. He used Donna as a sex object and got rid of her when she wouldn't continue in that role after he married a young society woman from a well-to-do family.

Now some happy circumstances had come along that caused Dwayne and Donna Sue to get together again. This joyful event occurred after she discovered the positive changes in his attitude toward his way of life. He also had a hell of a lot of money. He was even able to provide her with a car and took care of the upkeep, insurance and other expenses of the vehicle. She was happy with this new

Dwayne Wheeler, but wasn't fully convinced he wouldn't slide back into his old ways.

Dwayne turned away from the window and walked down the hall to the F.B.I. office. Agent Steve Williams' receptionist Ruth Henderson looked up at his entrance. "Good morning, Mister Wheeler," she greeted. "Mister Williams said I was to send you in to see him the moment you arrived."

When he stepped into the office he stopped in surprise. Besides Williams there were two other men with him. Dwayne asked, "What's going on?"

"Hello, Dwayne," Williams said. "Take a seat. This is Agent Larry Tomlinson and Mister David Arnsteiner. There is an international case in the works that is right up your alley. The Bureau has issued an official okay to hire you for a special job."

Dwayne noticed Arnsteiner was obviously a foreigner from his appearance. The guy looked as if he might be a cop or maybe a criminal who was rolling over to avoid a long prison sentence.

Williams sensed Dwayne's uneasiness. "Mister Arnsteiner is a German Jew. When the war broke out he was living in Palestine as a Zionist."

"What's a Zionist?"

Arnsteiner interjected, "We are Jews who wish to establish a homeland in Palestine. Because of the war in Europe, I joined a formation called the Jewish Battalion that was commanded by British officers."

"Oh," Dwayne commented. "That's all pretty Jewish all right."

Arnsteiner continued, "I fought in Greece and Italy."

"Okay," Dwayne said. He turned to Williams. "Where do I fit in?"

Tomlinson spoke up. "I can explain it to you, but I

won't give you all the finer details until you agree to take on the assignment."

Dwayne was not enthusiastic and he looked at Williams once again. "Is this another undercover caper? The last one you stuck me on almost got me killed."

Williams stated, "Listen to Tomlinson."

The F.B.I. agent began, "A lot of personal property in occupied Europe was stolen by the Nazis during the war. This included very expensive items that had once belonged to Jews who were killed in the concentration camps and luckier ones who escaped to other countries. Are you familiar with the situation?"

"I saw Dachau concentration camp. I was in the military police."

"Then you were stationed in Europe, so you're familiar with what went on there," Tomlinson went on. "Mister Arnsteiner has a personal interest in the situation since he lost his entire family at Auschwitz. But he was able to recover his former home in Germany. However, all the furniture and other valuables were gone. I'll let him elaborate."

Arnsteiner lit a cigarette, then began his clarification. "There were five very valuable paintings in the house where I spent my boyhood. They are gone of course, having disappeared with other similar works of art that once belonged to Jewish victims. I am part of an organization that has been working to recover such treasures. We discovered through a sympathetic young German's efforts that many painting masterpieces have somehow gotten into Wichita."

Dwayne's detective instincts kicked in. "How and when did he do that?"

"He obtained an important document and turned it over to us. It revealed the Wichita connection. But nobody knows where or who in this city is holding them."

Dwayne suddenly felt as if he'd just been slapped across the face with a wet towel, but tried to appear as if only slightly interested.

Williams joined in the conversation. "You have a good reputation when it comes to dealing with crime in this city. All we are asking for you to do is check among your contacts to see if anybody had been fencing valuables from Europe." He paused, noticing Dwayne seemed a tad nervous about something. "Are you willing to take the assignment?"

Dwayne knew if he refused, it would seem peculiar enough to be suspicious. "Ah...sure. I can do this. No problem."

Williams gave him a closer look. "Have you been in a fight?"

"Yeah," Dwayne answered. "I was hired by a bail bondsman to pick up a jumper. The guy was big and mean and resented our invitation to return to jail with us."

Williams laughed. "I hope you were well paid for the job."

"Oh, sure. I'm just rolling in dough."

"Okay," Williams noted. "We learned you moved in on the second floor directly below. You are now known as the Wheeler Detective Agency, aren't you?"

"The one and only," Dwayne said. "I can start an investigation tomorrow morning. Who's paying me?"

"The United States Government," Tomlinson answered. "I believe you're familiar with their generosity in something as important as this."

Arnsteiner said, "And our organization will give you a bonus if you succeed in your efforts. And I can now disclose a name that we have not revealed. He is deeply involved in this case."

Tomlinson was angry. "We were told you and your organization had not kept any information from us."

"I am *not* going to apologize for that," Arnsteiner snapped. He glanced at Dwayne. "His name is Nigel Hawthorne and he is a disgraced British Army officer."

Dwayne felt a hard nervous twitch in his stomach as he stood up. "Okay. I'll start tomorrow morning visiting a couple of fences I know around town. I'll check in with you later."

"Great!" Williams said. "In the meantime I'll have a contract drawn up for you."

The shamus hurried down to his office, then slowed his pace as he approached the door. He walked in as casually as possible. Donna Sue looked up. "What's going on?"

"It's a Federal case involving some stolen property that's supposed to have ended up here in Wichita," he answered. "They want me to dig around and see if I can find out what's going on." He paused. "Didn't you say you had to go to the beauty parlor this morning? I'll make some phone calls while you're gone. We can go out to the Continental Grill for lunch after you get back."

"Great idea," Donna Sue said, grabbing her purse. "I'll only be a couple of hours at the most."

She left and Dwayne waited until he heard the elevator whine downward, then reached out to the phone and picked up the receiver. He dialed the operator and asked for long distance. When connected, he gave Pete Van Dyke's number in New York City.

Sybil Van Dyke responded to the call with a simple, "Hello."

"Hi, Sybil. It's me, Dwayne. I gotta speak to Pete right away. Tell him it's important. *Real* important!"

A moment later Pete came on the line. "Hello, Dwayne. What's got you so excited?"

"Listen, Pete. You told me that art cabal was on the up and up, didn't you?"

"Sure did."

Dwayne gritted his teeth then spoke rapidly. "Then why the fuck does the F.B.I. want me to dig up where the stuff might be hid here in Wichita?"

"Jesus Christ! What's going on, Dwayne?"

"I got called into the local F.B.I. office a few minutes ago. There was a Jewish guy there who was in the Lions Club or something and—"

Pete interrupted. "The Lions Club?"

"Yeah, I think that's what he said. He was in Palestine in the Lions."

"Are you sure he didn't say Zionist?"

"Ah!" Dwayne exclaimed. "Yeah. That's it. A Zionist. At any rate, he ended up in the British Army and fought against the Germans. After the war he went home and found out his family had died in a concentration camp and he got his house back. But all the valuables were stolen by the Krauts during the war and that included five valuable paintings."

"I don't see how that has anything to do with the Cabal."

"The guy mentioned Nigel Hawthorne."

"Oh, shit," Pete said. "Just a minute, Dwayne. Let me think." A half minute passed and he could be heard clearing his throat a couple of times between taking deep breaths. "Okay. Let me lay it out for you. You've learned the truth. There is no cabal. Those paintings we're

handling are going to be used by former *Waffen-SS* officers. I don't know what for."

Dwayne was stunned. "We're working for the
goddamn German *Waffen-SS*? They're the fucking
enemy, Pete. Remember all the shit we saw in France and
Belgium and Holland because of those bastards?
Remember Dachau? You and me were there together.
Remember all them poor dead people laid out in stacks?"

"Yes, I remember. But there's a lot of money in this.
What about those two hundred bucks a week you're earning. Don't start going noble on me, Dwayne."

"I want out!"

"You're not getting out of this art deal, Dwayne! And
let me warn you. Any dumb stunts on your part can prove
fatal for both you and Donna Sue!"

"Aw, man! You got me in some deep shit, Pete!"

"Look now. Calm down. There's no problem. Just
carry on for the F.B.I. and draw out your investigation. As
soon as you get the word to mail those tubes, take care of
it. That'll be the end of the deal and I promise there will
be a big bonus that'll blow your mind. You know what
kind of a guy Nigel is."

"Okay. I got no choice."

"Good," Pete said. "I'll be in touch. Don't worry."

Dwayne hung up the phone. "Man oh man!" he
uttered aloud. "I really gotta keep this from Donna Sue."

CHAPTER 29

From the first day of their renewed romance, Dwayne and Donna Sue wanted to share an apartment. The problem they faced was that Kansas blue laws prohibited unmarried couples cohabiting. In fact, if discovered, the offending couple would be declared joined in a common-law marriage and would need to go through a divorce if they wanted to end their relationship. Consequently, Donna Sue had to keep her apartment even though she spent every night sleeping over with Dwayne. His building manager Toby Stafford knew all about their situation. But as long as Donna Sue had another apartment he wasn't concerned about her actually living with Dwayne.

The inconvenience of their situation was solved unexpectedly when a renter living in a small apartment down the hall from Dwayne, vacated the residence. Toby quickly let Dwayne and Donna Sue know about it. The empty apartment was offered and accepted making their living arrangements more convenient.

It took four trips with both cars to move Donna Sue's

belongings to her new place. She didn't have any furniture but had pots and pans, dishes, flatware, bedding and other items. When all her property had been placed in the new apartment, most of her clothing was stowed in the closet since space was limited at Dwayne's. The items she wouldn't need were left in boxes stacked in the smaller apartment. Her toiletries and other personal items were taken to his bedroom and bathroom.

The day after settling in, Dwayne realized they wouldn't need two cars, He took the Buick to a used car lot and sold it. He knew the crafty dealer cheated him outrageously on the price, but without the expenses of upkeep and insurance on the vehicle, he figured things would eventually even out.

———

A COUPLE OF DAYS LATER DWAYNE AND DONNA Sue had just opened the Wheeler Detective Agency for the day when a man stepped into the small reception area. Donna Sue gave him a polite smile and asked what he needed.

"I would like to speak to Mister Dwayne Wheeler."

"Of course, sir." She pressed the button on the unnecessary but impressive intercom. "Mister Wheeler, a gentleman is out here wishing to see you."

Dwayne, with an expression of cool confidence on his face, appeared. "What can I do for you, sir?"

The man handed him a document. "Please take a look at this."

Dwayne opened the paper then growled. "You son of a bitch! This is a court summons!"

The process server, used to such reactions, smiled, tipped his hat and withdrew.

Donna Sue was alarmed. "What did he give you?"

"Me and A.J. are getting sued for a hunnerd thousand dollars!"

She stood up in alarm. "I don't understand!"

"The plaintiff is Freddy Baldwin who is claiming we injured him without reason when we took him into custody. The words in this thing include *reckless, uncontrolled, vicious* and other such bullshit."

"And they want a hundred thousand dollars?"

"Well, they're asking for more'n they expect to be awarded," Dwayne explained. "The most they could get would prob'ly be seventy-five thousand bucks."

"Oh! That takes a load off my mind," she responded sarcastically.

"Me and A.J. will split it even-steven if we lose."

"My! It keeps getting better and better, doesn't it?" The phone suddenly rang and she picked it up. "Wheeler Detective Agency...yes, he's right here."

"I bet that's A.J.," Dwayne said. He took the phone. "I know what you're calling about."

A.J. said, "Yeah. You were served, huh? Okay, I suggest we call on our go-to guy Carl Banter."

"Good idea," Dwayne agreed. "He's been a damn good lawyer for us a couple of times in the past."

"I'll set us up an appointment."

Dwayne hung up. "I gotta go upstairs and let Steve Williams in on this."

He hurried down to the stairwell and took the steps two and three at a time up to the third floor. When he rushed into the F.B.I. office, Ruth Henderson was slightly alarmed. "Anything wrong, Mister Wheeler?"

"Yeah. I gotta see Steve. Now!"

Miss Henderson spoke into the intercom, then nodded an acquiescence to Dwayne. He went through the door and blurted. "I'm getting sued. For a hunnerd thousand dollars."

"Whoa!" Steve Williams said. "Calm down and let me in on this."

"Remember when I told you about working with the bondsman A.J. Kessler? Well, the guy we took into custody is suing us for beating him up."

"Did you two beat him up?"

"We sure as hell did because the big son of a bitch was resisting us," Dwayne explained. "So it looks like I'm gonna have to delay my investigation into the local connection to Jewish valuables."

Williams shook his head. "Nope. The Bureau isn't going to like that." He slid a paper across his desk. "Here's your contract to look for Jewish treasures. Sign it!"

"Not now! I got too much hanging over my head!"

"You obligated yourself in the presence of two F.B.I. agents, Dwayne. And this case must be pursued with timely aggression."

"Me and A.J. have a court date, Steve! He's got insurance for stuff like this. I don't. He's making an appointment with our lawyer."

"I understand your predicament," Williams said. "So go on and get an attorney and I'll get back to you. But you are going to give the majority of your attention to this Wichita connection."

"I will," Dwayne promised. "Just keep in mind I'm in deep shit where this suit is concerned. If we lose, I'm wiped out. And it'll prob'ly cost me my P.I. license."

"I appreciate the risk," Steve stated. "I'll be in touch."

———

CARL BANTER'S LAW OFFICE WAS LOCATED IN the Central Building at Douglas and Main. This was three blocks north of A.J.'s office. When A.J. called Banter and explained the lawsuit, the attorney wasted no time in setting up an appointment for mid-afternoon of that same day.

Now Dwayne and A.J. sat in front of Banter's desk. The little man's short legs weren't far past the seat of the chair on which he had deftly climbed onto. He had a briefcase in which he'd brought all the paperwork on the Baldwin case. Dwayne had no work record of the incident even in his own files. He thought it was going to be cut-and-dried like all the other incidents of running down bail jumpers.

Banter was a slim, balding serious forty-year-old who had a good reputation in Sedgwick County as a criminal lawyer. He scrutinized A.J.'s record of the Baldwin apprehension. After fifteen minutes of a careful read he turned his attention to his clients. "I have some questions. Did either or both of you actually attack Baldwin?"

"Well," Dwayne replied, "It was at night and we discovered he was asleep in a bedroom. We snuck in and I jumped on top of him on the bed as soon as A.J. turned on the light switch."

"No you didn't," Banter stated.

"Yes I did."

"I'll tell you what happened," Banter spoke implicitly. "You and A.J. went in just like his report says. But when A.J. switched on the light, Baldwin charged you."

Dwayne quickly caught on. "Yeah! The big son of a bitch attacked me."

Banter gave an affirmative nod. "And he hit you so hard you were slammed against a chest of drawers. You bounced off that piece of heavy furniture and then he punched you in the jaw, and you fell to the floor."

"Sure. I remember that."

Banter looked at A.J. "At that point in the struggle, Baldwin turned his attention on you. He is an extremely large, tall and broad man and you knew he had the ability to inflict serious injuries on you. Even death. So you hit him across the shoulders and chest with the baton. In your haste and fear, you also accidently struck him in the genitals."

A.J. grinned. "That's absolutely correct."

"And at that point, this dangerous fugitive was done in."

"Right," Dwayne said. "We cuffed him and put a hog-tie harness on him and carried him out to the car."

"No!" Banter stated. "You two cuffed him, then *walked* him out to the car."

Dwayne winked. "I thought that was what I said. We *walked* him out to the car."

Banter went over the paperwork again. "We're going up against Andy Fawcett. He's one oily son of a bitch. But we'll give him a good fight, I promise."

"There's one other thing, Carl," A.J. said. "Baldwin is still in Saint Francis hospital."

"Let's keep in mind that all it involves is a simple majority of the jury to either acquit or find you guilty."

Dwayne groaned.

CHAPTER 30

Later that same week Dwayne was called to Steve Williams' office for a two o'clock meeting. The shamus had anticipated that such sessions would occur and prepared for it by keeping a pseudo-diary of investigative activity on the art project.

He decided to show the F.B.I. agent at least one real contact. He had enough time to see Pete Driscoll before reporting to Steve Williams.

———

PETE DRISCOLL HAD GIVEN HIM EVIDENCE TO solve the murder of a bookie by the name of Stub Durham during the Kansas City takeover caper. Dwayne didn't like Pete much even though the guy had done him that big favor. Pete dealt in stolen goods ranging from refrigerators to jewelry with a plethora of other valuable items in between. Dwayne had no respect for fences who bought and sold somebody else's property. The buyers were as bad as the thieves as far as he was concerned.

Dwayne arranged to see Pete and drove to one of their meeting places in a shopping center at Hillside and Pawnee. He parked off to the side of the lot and waited fifteen minutes until Pete showed up. Dwayne walked over and got into the fence's Cadillac.

"Hey, Pete."

"Hey, Dwayne. Are you selling or buying?"

"Neither. I'm trying to locate some paintings."

The shamus carried on the interview as if he were really searching for stolen art. Pete, of course, knew nothing but promised to notify him if he got wind of any such loot. "I got to tell you something, Dwayne. I handle valuable commodities, but nothing fancy like artistic masterpieces. That's way out of my line."

"I know, but keep your eyes and ears open, okay?"

Dwayne returned to the Nash, and drove off, fully realizing that the art cabal angle meant he had been dealing in stolen property. To make it worse, the loot had been taken by Nazis who had murdered the former owners.

———

Dwayne checked in with Miss Henderson at Williams' office a few minutes past two o'clock. She announced him on the intercom, and he went through the door into William's bailiwick and saw that Agent Larry Tomlinson and the Zionist David Arnsteiner were both present. He grabbed a chair and took a seat, nodding greetings to the three men.

Steve Williams wasted no time. "What've you got to report, Dwayne?"

Dwayne took out his notebook in which he'd written down the confab with Pete as well as several made-up inquiries around Wichita. He gave the list a quick scan then said, "I don't have much to report. I visited four guys I know that deal in stolen goods. None had any information on painted pictures. And they ain't heard rumors about anything like that going on in Wichita."

"I'm not surprised," Williams said. "And I'd like the names of your points of contact."

Dwayne shook his head. "I can't do it, Steve. These are guys on the street that keep me informed when I need 'em. If I revealed them, I'd lose some good sources of information."

Tomlinson wasn't buying that. "We need those names, Dwayne."

"Client protection," Dwayne firmly stated. "The law's on my side. I gave you Pete Driscoll's name because he's pretty well known around town. But you can cross him off any list of suspects."

Williams was interested. "Isn't he the witness that informed you who killed that bookie a couple of years back?"

"Yeah."

Tomlinson wasn't giving up. "Did you give him a thorough interrogation?"

Dwayne snorted a chuckle. "Pete is what you'd call cunning, Larry. Ever'body in Wichita knows his background. But nobody—including the F.B.I.—has ever found out how he operates or where he stashes his goods. And that includes how he disposes of 'em."

"Dwayne's right," Williams said. "The guy's been picked up by the Wichita P.D. countless times, but never stayed in custody more than a couple of hours."

David Arnsteiner asked, "Is it not possible for this criminal to be arrested in the middle of the night? Then taken somewhere and given a vigorous interrogation."

Williams shook his head. "Pete Driscoll's operations aren't a threat to the security of the United States. As a common criminal, he is protected by the Constitution."

Dwayne lit a Lucky Strike. "I'm beginning to think there ain't anybody in Wichita that's in this caper. Even when you guys hired me, I felt like it was a dead-end job."

Arnsteiner countered, "I personally saw the *SS* organization's document that emphatically states that stolen artwork has been sent to this city."

"Okay," Dwayne said. "Don't worry. I'll dig deeper."

"By the way," Williams said, "how's that lawsuit going?"

"A.J. and I hired Carl Banter to represent us."

"I know Carl. He's a damn good lawyer."

Larry Tomlinson was curious. "What's this all about?"

Dwayne explained, "I was hired by a bondsman friend of mine to go with him to bring in a bail jumper. It turned into a brawl and now the guy is suing us for beating the shit out of him." He chuckled. "Our defense is that he also beat the shit out of us."

Once more Arnsteiner was confused. "I assume the man whom you and your friend apprehended was a criminal, was he not?"

"He damn sure was," Dwayne replied. "As a matter of fact, he's been in and out of jail ever since he was a kid."

"I see. So this criminal is suing you for money because of fighting while he was being arrested?"

"That's what's the matter."

"I would like to see a copy of the United States Constitution," Arnsteiner said. "This is all very confusing for me."

"Don't bother," Tomlinson advised him. "It's like the Bible. It can be interpreted in countless ways."

———

THE PRAIRIE WIND GOLF AND TENNIS CLUB
was where Wichita society's *crème de la crème* gathered together for recreation, exercise, dining and posh social events. There were also activities held at the club where local civic organizations and charities got together to arrange campaigns to benefit the less fortunate of the city. It was also a great spot for businessmen to hash out various deals among themselves.

This latter purpose was why Deputy District Attorney Bob Delaney was in the dining room sitting at a table during the serving of lunch. He sipped a martini as he waited for another member he had invited to join him. He looked up when a man walked in, noting it was Attorney Andy Fawcett. Delaney raised his hand and signaled to the lawyer.

Fawcett walked over and joined him. "How are you, Bob?"

"Fine, Andy. How're things going for you?"

"Couldn't be better," Fawcett stated. "I was surprised to receive your invitation. Is there anything special going on?"

"Let's eat first," Delaney suggested. He raised his hand one more time to signal a waiter that they were ready to see the luncheon menus. From that point on, both men concentrated on small talk, eating lunch and having another serving of cocktails.

Fawcett was feeling the effect of the alcohol. "I'm curious as to why Sedgwick County is treating me to lunch."

"Andy, I must tell you that it isn't the county that's feeding us. It's the Federal Government."

Fawcett's eyes opened wide. "Really? And how did this come about?"

"It involves the lawsuit you've brought against the bondsman A.J. Kessler and the private detective Dwayne Wheeler." He shifted in his chair and leaned forward. "That suit is not going forward."

"And why not?"

"Because it is frivolous and will not end up in your client's favor."

Fawcett grinned. "Now what makes you think that, Bob?"

"It is a fiasco that will interfere with the prosecution of Freddy Baldwin," Delaney explained. Fawcett started to speak but the deputy D.A. interrupted. "You know damn well you can't possibly win the case. You talked the Newly couple into letting you file it so you could milk some more money out of them."

Fawcett frowned. "I resent that, Bob! And I want to know why the Feds are tied up in this situation."

"I don't know. But if you proceed, the district attorney will file charges against you for—as I said—a frivolous lawsuit with no merit. That might result in the Newly family suing you for malpractice."

Fawcett sat in silence for a moment. "I give up. You win. Tell your boss I have surrendered." He stood up. "It was nice having lunch with you, Bob."

Fawcett left, and once more Delaney summoned a waiter. "Bring me a telephone please." After the instrument was placed in front of him, he dialed a number. As soon as Miss Ruth Henderson answered, Delaney said, "Ruth, tell Steve Williams that the lawsuit involving Dwayne Wheeler has been withdrawn. Thank you."

He hung up and ordered another martini. After all, the F.B.I. would be paying for it.

CHAPTER 31

Attorney Andy Fawcett, carrying a briefcase, walked into the Newly Machine Shop on George Washington Boulevard just south of Pawnee Street. He entered a short hallway leading down to the noisy portion of the business where the lathes, drill presses and other machinery were creating a deafening roar. The office shared by Willard and Clara Newly was off to one side of the building. The couple could be seen through a large plate-glass window that gave them an excellent view of the work area.

Fawcett opened the office door and stepped in. When he closed it, he noticed the room had been soundproofed to keep the noise of the machinery down to a minimum. Both Willard and Clara, sitting at their desks on opposite sides of the room, were surprised to see him.

"What's going on, Andy?" Willard asked.

"I have some news." There were chairs along the wall and Fawcett grabbed one, situating it between them. He sat down with the briefcase in his lap. "A very unexpected and irritating hitch has come up."

Clara, with an open ledger in front of her, put down the pencil she had been using to enter payroll data. She looked up with a frown. "Anything the matter?"

"I'm afraid it is just as I stated. I was contacted by the Sedgwick County District Attorney's office and told that our lawsuit has been disallowed."

Willard was puzzled. "Why?"

"They said it was frivolous under the circumstances. That..."He paused to begin his alibi. "...that since Freddy had a warrant out for his arrest and had a criminal record...well...that the county wasn't going to go to the expense of a civil trial that was unwinnable."

"Can they do that?" Clara asked.

"They *have* done it," Fawcett replied.

"Well, hell!" Willard growled. He glowered at Clara. "That goddamn brother of yours had been nothing but trouble and a disappointment for us through our whole marriage."

"It's not his fault!" Clara exclaimed. "Daddy was always mean to him when he was a boy."

Willard countered, "He was mean to him because *Freddy* was mean! He'd even been caught taking lunch money from other kids at school. And there was that string of burglaries."

"Let's not worry about the civil case now," Fawcett counseled. "The criminal trial is gonna be a humdinger and that means I'll be fighting long and hard for the Newly family."

"Goddamn it!" Willard cursed. "This isn't the *Newly* family's concern. It's the *Baldwin's* family problem. But we have to pay for it."

"That reminds me," Fawcett said, opening the briefcase and pulling out a sheet of paper. "Here's my invoice for the civil trial."

Clara spoke up loudly. "I thought you said there wasn't gonna be a civil trial."

"I did. But I had to draw up papers and file them. I paid the fees, too, out of my own pocket. This was all done before the proceedings were canceled."

Willard, always careful with a dime, protested, "But since the county stopped the trial. We shouldn't have to pay you nothing!"

Fawcett was used to this reaction and had a reply he had made many times. "Well, normally I'd bill you, but since there's gonna be a criminal trial, I'll forget about it." He knew he could pad the cost of defending Freddy Baldwin to get enough money to pay for his expenses in making the civil application. He stood up. "I'm going to visit Freddy at the hospital and bring him up to date on things. I'll see you later."

"Okay," Willard said, "And thanks for not charging us."

"Think nothing of it," Fawcett said.

He left the office and headed for the exit, grimacing against the loud noise.

———

DAVID ARNSTEINER WAS EVENTUALLY LODGED IN the F.B.I. safehouse on Nineteenth Street near the river in the Riverside district of Wichita. The site was in a tree-lined pleasant neighborhood of middle-class homes. Arnsteiner wondered why the neighbors were not overly curious about the unknown use of the large house in their midst. John Mikowski, the head of the security detail assigned to the location, explained that the local residents were made to believe that Boeing, Beech and other aircraft manufacturers in Wichita used it as a place to board government visitors. They were further informed that a lot of important government dealing went on there. Thus the various comings and goings of strangers were eventually ignored by the locals.

On his first morning, Arnsteiner awoke early and went down to the kitchen for breakfast. The cook greeted him with a nod of his head. "How d'you want your eggs?"

Arnsteiner shrugged. "Scrambled, I suppose."

"You want bacon with that?"

Arnsteiner was amused that as a Jew he was being offered bacon. He noticed some fried potatoes in a skillet. "No bacon, but those will suffice. Thank you very much."

He joined three other men at the table. The only words spoken were quick salutations, then the consumption of food continued. The others left one by one to begin their day's activities. Arnsteiner finished eating fifteen minutes later and got up, walking toward the door.

"Don't forget to sign out on the sheet by the door, sir," the cook reminded him. "And remember to put down the time and where you're going."

Arnsteiner, noticing the others had signed out as per the directive, replied, "I thought I would take a walk around the neighborhood for some exercise. Is that all right?"

"That's fine, sir. You are free to leave the house but stay close by."

Arnsteiner walked over and noted that his breakfast companions had all gone to different places. He scribbled down his signature, the time and wrote in "local area" before he left the house. He went down the driveway to the sidewalk, turning in the direction of some stores located along a nearby street. The Zionist had noticed the location when he was driven to the safehouse.

Arnsteiner was secretly downcast and worried about

the way things were going. The detective Wheeler seemed competent enough, but his lack of success indicated the paintings were in deep concealment that might end up making it impossible to locate them. The Jew walked down to the shopping area and spotted a public telephone outside a cafe. He went over and stepped into the booth, pulling a slip of paper bearing a phone number from the lining of his coat. After putting a nickel in the phone slot he dialed.

The call was answered by a masculine voice. "Hello."

Arnsteiner spoke in Hebrew. "*Ma shlomkah?*"

The voice replied in the same language, "I am fine. Except I have headaches."

That completed the challenge and password. Arnsteiner still speaking Hebrew said, "I am now living in the F.B.I. safehouse. Do you know where it is?"

"Yes."

"I am standing in front of a cafe at the corner of Nineteenth Street and Burns Avenue," Arnsteiner informed him. "Can you meet me here?"

"I can be there in about twenty minutes," the stranger said. "I will be wearing a brown leather jacket and a fedora hat."

Arnsteiner hung up and began slowly pacing up and down the street. He didn't want to be cornered inside a small cafe if things went bad. After a few long minutes passed, a 1930s Ford sedan pulled up to the curb. Arnsteiner moved cautiously toward it, watching a man in a leather jacket get out. Then he recognized him.

"Dani!" Arnsteiner exclaimed.

Dani Epstein's jaw dropped. He spoke in English, saying. "David Arnsteiner! I cannot believe it!"

The two had served together in the Jewish Brigade from its inception to the end of the war. They embraced in a masculine, back-pounding manner, laughing with delight. Arnsteiner asked, "What are you doing here in this city?"

Epstein spoke softly. "I am a Zionist agent. That is it, plain and simple. We have a small headquarters in Washington. I was sent here as a contact, but I never dreamed it would be you."

"We are attracting attention out here," Arnsteiner said. "Let us go into the cafe for some coffee."

The two entered the small establishment and found it empty except for the proprietor behind the counter. They took a booth in the back and the owner walked up to them. "What can I get you guys?"

"Coffee, please," Epstein replied.

"I got some cherry pie and apple pie fresh in this morning. Can I interest you in a piece?"

"I would like apple," Epstein answered

"Same for me, please," Arnsteiner said.

The owner went back to tend to the order, and Epstein turn to his companion. "The people here have a saying that goes 'There is nothing more American than apple pie.'"

Arnsteiner grinned. "Then we are following local custom."

The owner served them each a slab of pie and a cup of coffee from a tray he carried to their booth. Then he went back to his position behind the counter. Arnsteiner and Epstein carried on a lighthearted conversation in Hebrew bringing each other up to date on what had happened since they'd last been together.

Epstein took a last bite of his pie, then asked, "How are things going?"

"I take it you know what I am looking for."

"Yes. The situation with stolen paintings hidden here

was revealed to us and we learned the *Tsad'yod-mem* was involved. My boss was contacted by Yitzhak Cohen with authorization to lend a hand."

"I am glad to hear that, Dani. The F.B.I. has me worried. I am certain they are waiting for the right opportunity to move in and take over the project."

"The American government is using Nazis in their espionage against the Soviet Union. Their excuse is that those Germans had a lot of experience fighting the Russians. That means they do not want us Jews to take revenge on them. However, the Americans approve of having a Jewish State established in Palestine." He paused for a sip of coffee. "Now tell me about how things are going here in Wichita."

"There is a private detective here who is much admired by the F.B.I.," Arnsteiner replied. "They have used him in the past and evidently the man is an expert and has many connections with the underworld of this city. He has the ability to dig up information and clues even more than the police."

"Mmm," Epstein mused. "That is an excellent situation."

"The only problem is that I feel he is not being supervised enough."

"Americans are not like Europeans, David. They do not need nor do they want too much supervision in their undertakings. They work best when left alone."

"That does not ease my apprehension."

"Then I have good news for you. Arrangements can easily be made to keep him under surveillance. You will be pleased to learn we have an undercover team here in Wichita just for that purpose. They came out with me from Washington."

Arnsteiner finished his pie. "I must insist that their duties are coordinated with me. Without fail."

"As you wish, my friend. It's a nice day, so let's go over to the park and sit down on a bench. As old veterans we can reminisce about our time in the Jewish Brigade."

CHAPTER 32

Dwayne had given his current situation a lot of serious thought. He knew if he revealed the truth about the phony art cabal to Donna Sue she would come unglued. And if he told her about the Nazis and stolen goods from Jews who died in the concentration camps, she would go completely ballistic. Thus, the shamus made two decisions; the first was to keep mum about the circumstances and the second was to go out and do some real investigating even if he knew there was nothing to be found. By doing that he could bring back proof of negative results to cover his ass.

Since he had already visited the fence Pete Driscoll, he prowled Wichita, going to other fences, pawn shops, and even a gang who dealt in stolen auto parts. The automobile racketeers responded to his investigation by laughing at his inquiries regarding masterpiece paintings instead of carburetors, generators, radiators or other car parts. Even if he was bullshitting them, Dwayne resented their ridicule and haughtily stated, "I am leaving no stone unturned."

One of the guys laughed. "I don't think you're gonna find any painted pitchers under rocks, Dwayne."

The shamus decided to end the day's investigation with a visit to Lieutenant Ben Forester of the Wichita Police Department. This guy was one cop he could trust and, although the officer worked in homicide, he would have inside information on burglary cases through inter-departmental crime reports. Listing an interview with the police lieutenant on his bogus information would impress the F.B.I. and Arnsteiner.

Dwayne walked into the homicide office past the desk of his nemesis Sergeant Al Gallagher. They glanced at each other and exchanged scowls. Dwayne and Gallagher had developed a deep hatred for each other through clashes of their very diverse personalities over the years.

Lieutenant Forester, on the other hand, had a great deal of respect for Dwayne's detective's skills in crime solving. Dwayne had proved a valuable asset through his thorough knowledge of Wichita's underworld.

Dwayne walked over to the other side of the office and rapped on Forester's door and stepped inside. "How're you doing, Ben?"

Forester looked up from studying a report on a murder investigation still in progress. "Hey there, Dwayne. What's up?"

"I'm on a special burglary investigation and need some information," Dwayne replied, sitting down on a chair at the side of the policeman's desk.

"Then go down to burglary."

"Can't do it, Ben. This is highly sensitive stuff."

"I see. Who's your client?"

"Ask me no questions and...well, you know how that old saying goes."

"Then what can I do for you?"

"I'd be real happy if you'd run through the file of burglary reports for the past year."

"I'm real busy, Dwayne. What's been burgled?"

"Paintings. Old masterpiece paintings."

"Those kinds of break-ins, etcetera are in a special file all their own," Forester said. He went to a cabinet and came back with a manila folder. He opened it and began going through the dozen reports inside.

Dwayne relaxed in the chair beside the lieutenant's desk gazing around the room, noting a half dozen plaques that his cop friend had earned during his career. The policeman thumbed through a thick number of burglary reports.

"Nope," Forester said. "No paintings. There's an ancient Chinese vase, valuable antiques, some jewelry and ...oh! Here's one on your ex-girlfriend's jewelry."

"We're back together again. And she got robbed of some pretty expensive stuff."

"I know you have a legal obligation not to reveal the names of your clients, but what are the details that you can tell me about?"

Dwayne shook his head and stood up. "Sorry, Ben. Thanks for the favor, huh?"

"I hope to hell you aren't digging yourself into a deep hole. You still jump from side-to-side over the lines of legality and illegality."

"Give me a break, Ben."

"Y'know it's a shame about your army discharge keeping you from becoming a regular police officer. You would've made a first class homicide detective."

Dwayne grinned and winked, then left the office and headed for the door. He came to an abrupt halt beside Gallagher's desk. "Why, hello, Sergeant Gallagher. You're looking quite spiffy this morning."

"Fuck you, shamus."

Dwayne laughed and headed for the exit.

———

DAVID ARNSTEINER AND DANI EPSTEIN MET again in the Riverside neighborhood. This time it was at a bench looking out over the Arkansas River. Arnsteiner had discovered Chesterfield cigarettes and lit one. He had also purchased several cartons to take back with him to Europe.

Arnsteiner muttered in Hebrew, "I am beginning to think this whole thing is a waste of time."

"Do not become discouraged, David. There are a number of unknowns involved that are deeply hidden. It is not like when we were in the Jewish Brigade and could quickly find the enemy then attack."

"I realize that my impatience is due to wanting to find the five paintings stolen from my home in Germany. But as I told you, I do not think the Investigator Wheeler is under enough instruction or supervision. The man simply goes out on his own every few days and comes back with negative reports."

"I see," Epstein said. "What do those reports say?"

"That is the crux of the problem. I am denied access to any of the documents regarding this activity."

"As I told you before, the Americans are that way. When involved in an operation, they keep everything to themselves. The F.B.I. is particularly sensitive about what they reveal or know." He paused. "And so are we. I think this is the time when I can reveal what our Zionist organization can do for you."

Arnsteiner frowned in combined surprise and anger. "You are informing me at this late date?"

"Do not blame me, David. I have my orders, too. At any rate, we have that undercover team for surveillance and bodyguards I mentioned. I am authorized to grant your access to them."

"Excellent! The most important thing they must do is keep tabs on that private investigator."

"It is all up to you, my friend," Epstein said. "What do you say to going to that restaurant for some pie? Then I shall make arrangements for what you need."

CHAPTER 33

I t was late when Dwayne returned to his apartment and found Donna Sue waiting for him. She noticed how tired he looked. "Hard day?"

"Monotonous mostly."

He had actually been driving around the city trying to put things straight in his mind. That thought process made him realize that there was a strong possibility this caper would eventually collapse into a personal catastrophe. And it would not only affect him but Donna Sue as well. He had plenty of money to afford an elaborate dropping out-of-sight, but would need more if they wanted to disappear for an extended period of time in a comfortable place.

Donna Sue sensed the apprehension in his voice. "You seem to have gotten a lot on your mind since you left the apartment this morning."

"I think enough time has passed to sell your jewels. I need to make arrangements to meet with Pete Driscoll."

Donna Sue gave him a suspicious look. "What's up, Dwayne?"

"Since I have the time to contact Pete, it makes sense to get it over with. The sooner we're rid of your jewels, the better it'll be. I'll give him a call from the office tomorrow."

"That's a good idea."

"Hey," Dwayne said. "I just realized I'm hungry. How's about we go to the Continental Grill for a late supper?"

"All right! I've been cooped up here in the apartment for most of the day."

"I knew you'd want to. I left the car at the curb instead of in the parking garage."

"You're a wise man, Dwayne Wheeler."

———

THE NEXT MORNING, AFTER DWAYNE AND Donna Sue arrived at the office, he put in a call to Pete Driscoll's number to make arrangement for a meeting. As usual it was answered by his helper Charlie. The fence's assistant said he'd inform Pete of the request, then abruptly hung up. He had orders from his boss to never linger on the telephone too long. Pete had a morbid fear of wiretaps.

A half hour later the office phone rang. Dwayne and Donna Sue were engaged in a game of cribbage at his desk. She laid her cards down and picked up the phone, answering with her scripted reply. "Wheeler Detective Agency. How may I direct your call?"

"Pete for Dwayne."

Donna Sue nodded to Dwayne. "It's Pete."

Dwayne took the handset. "Hey, Pete. I want a get-tOgether."

"Whatcha got?"

"Sparklers," Dwayne replied. "Expensive ones. Interested?"

"Linwood Park. West of the Canal. Park facing north on Hydraulic Street. Now."

"Gotcha."

————

DWAYNE WASTED NO TIME DRIVING TO THE rendezvous spot. He had the jewels in a briefcase beside him on the seat, and was also packing his .45 Colt semi-automatic. He and Pete Driscoll had an agreement that if they were ever hassled by an attempted arrest in a public place, Dwayne would immediately claim that the fence was a client. That gave them the right to keep mum about what they were doing.

The shamus sat patiently for twenty minutes then noted a car coming toward him in the rearview mirror. When it got closer he could see it was a new '48 Chrysler Windsor being driven by Charlie. He pulled up to the curb in front of Dwayne's station wagon.

Dwayne walked up to the Chrysler as Pete got out. Pete pointed to a park bench on a path a few yards away. They walked over in a casual manner and sat down.

Pete stated, "Gimme a quick rundown on the sparklers."

"They're Donna Sue's. They were burglarized from her apartment."

"By you?"

"By me."

"Insured?" Pete asked.

"Nope." Dwayne opened the briefcase and pulled out a velvet bag containing the jewels. He laid it in Pete's lap. The fence pulled a jeweler's glass from his jacket pocket and began examining the rings, bracelets, earrings and necklaces. There were a dozen objects for sale.

It took the fence only ten minutes to finish his assessment. "I'll take 'em all. What're you asking?"

"Ten grand."

Pete actually grinned. "Get real. One more time. What're you asking?"

"Ten grand," Dwayne repeated. "That's good stuff there. And remember; it ain't on any insurance company's records as stolen."

"I'm only inter'sted in the stones. I gotta break the pieces up." He paused for a moment. "A grand."

Now the bargaining turned serious. The two went back and forth, politely turning each other down. When the haggling was done, an agreed price of two thousand dollars had been reached. Pete waved to Charlie and motioned him to join them.

Dwayne had never learned Charlie's last name. He was a big guy, slow to talk but reportedly had no hesitation when it came to defending his boss. He was always packing a gun, knife and a sap loaded with ball-bearings. He stopped wordlessly and handed over a heavy brown envelope to Pete. The fence retrieved some bills from the cardboard container and counted out two thousand dollars.

The bargainers shook hands, and Dwayne stayed where he was as Pete and Charlie returned to the Chrysler. After they pulled away from the curb and went up Hydraulic Street, Dwayne walked over to his station wagon.

———

Deep in the inner recesses of the *Wolflager* three men sat at a table in an oak-paneled conference room. These were Nigel Hawthorne, Manfred von Leipinger and Franz Taubert. The remnants of a heavy supper of excellent black market food, delicacies and wine had been cleared away and the trio settled down to business.

Taubert pulled an expensive Cuban cigar from a humidor and passed the container over to his companions. He glanced at Hawthorne as the Englishman lit up. "How do you like living in Switzerland, Nigel?"

"A wonderful country," Hawthorne replied.

"The Alps are most beautiful in the winters. Before the war, I skied in Switzerland at least twice every year," Leipinger said. "Where is your home there?"

"That locale will remain my secret, Manfred. And I can't wait to get back after we discuss this latest situation."

"It is quite simple. It appears our operation is at an impasse, *nein*?"

Hawthorne returned his lighter to his inside jacket pocket. "An impasse, *ja*! But not to worry. In a way this may turn out to be advantageous for us."

Von Leipinger frowned. "I cannot agree with you, Nigel. Everything has come to a stop. It is an incalculable delay. You must keep in mind we do not have a lot of time to spend if we want our overall plan to succeed."

"We are in the midst of a minor difficulty," Hawthorne insisted. "We have over a million dollars' worth of art hidden away in the U.S.A. In reality, we are only dropping out of sight for awhile."

Taubert had his own worry. "I am not certain if we can trust that American detective for any length of time."

"I know the man quite well from working with him in

the past on another profitable and risky venture." The Englishman did not want to reveal the precarious operation had involved counterfeiting German military scrip to be exchanged for American dollars. It was a swindle foisted on the West German government. That might have sparked up a natural resentment from these German war veterans. "And my executive assistant was also involved in that deal. I have absolute trust in those two Americans. However, to ease your minds I'll contact my assistant and have him make a personal inspection of the stored paintings."

Von Leipinger shrugged. "We really have no choice in the matter. But at least the people who compromised you will not be able to trace your whereabouts. And you have the lovely Lale with you."

"True. Eventually things will settle down as our adversaries beat their heads against the numerous dead ends built into our campaign."

Taubert leaned forward, putting his elbows on the table. "If we end up facing any betrayals, those involved will be dealt a worst punishment than the officers who attempted to assassinate our *führer* Adolf Hitler."

"Indeed!" Von Leipinger exclaimed. "They were hanged from hooks by piano wire."

Taubert leaned back in his chair. "As you know we also have contacts in America the West German embassy, my dear Nigel. If your Americans fail us, we can easily be informed of their conduct by our men in Washington."

An orderly entered the room and sat down a tray containing a bottle of schnapps with three tumblers, then made a quick exit. Von Leipinger stood up and filled the glasses. "Shall we drink a toast to our impending victory?"

"*Natürlich,*" Taubert said, raising his glass. "*Sieg heil!*"

CHAPTER 34

D wayne and Donna Sue decided to celebrate the sale of the jewels with an evening at the Roadhouse night club. When he called in for reservations he asked for a table in the back of the room. He hoped the inconvenience of having to walk across the length of the building to the dance floor would keep Donna Sue's desires for tripping the light fantastic to a minimum.

After arriving, they had their usual brief but friendly conversation with the two doormen Jack Wallace and Denny Tarball. From there they went in to contact the Maître d' for the reservation to be checked off and a waitress assigned to them. The couple were pleased to see it was Teresa. She escorted them to the table where they ordered drinks and a snack mixture of pretzels and peanuts.

As soon as the waitress left to fetch the refreshments, Donna Sue frowned at Dwayne. "Is this the best table you could get?"

"Yeah. I was told it was too late to score one up front."

After the first round of refreshments, they wended

through the tables to dance. Dwayne suffered through three songs, then he hastily took Donna Sue's hand and led her back to their table before the orchestra could start playing again. Donna Sue was a little upset but not surprised. "I wish you'd learn to like dancing."

"I have *never* liked dancing. And I never *will* like dancing. Especially to the fast tunes."

Donna Sue smirked. "Party pooper! Wait! Here's a better description of you. Shindig shitter."

"Your vulgarity mortifies me."

"Excuse me, my darling," she said. "I forgot how easily upset you can get and I did not mean to agitate your delicate temperament."

Dwayne started to reply, but Teresa showed up to take their orders for another round of drinks. A moment later the club owner Elmer Pettibone stopped by to greet them. "I haven't seen you two for awhile. What've you been up to?"

"We have a new office in the W.K.H. building," Dwayne replied. "Donna Sue has joined me in the business. She takes care of all the administration stuff."

Pettibone was impressed. "Say! You're coming up in the world, ain't you?"

"Yes, we are, Elmer," Donna Sue said. "And Dwayne has some big plans for expanding the agency. It's going to take some time, but the hard work will be worth it."

"I'm sure," Pettibone said. "I wish you good luck."

Dwayne chuckled. "We'll need it."

The club owner walked away as Teresa showed up with the drinks and set them on the table. She also had another bowl of the mixed snack. "I'll be checking on you from time to time, but whenever you guys need anything, just wave your hands."

"Will do," Dwayne said.

As Teresa walked away, Donna Sue stood up and glared at Dwayne. "We're going to dance again. Come on!"

"Yes, ma'am."

———

Their private fête came to an end at one a.m. when they left the club to go home. Dwayne dropped Donna Sue off in front of the apartment house, then drove over to the parking garage to put the station wagon away. It was a short trip around to the other side of the block and he pulled into the entrance where the night watchman by the name of Fred manned the entrance/exit booth.

Fred was a retired Boeing machinist who had worked the graveyard shift all through the war. After leaving the company he found that no matter how hard he tried, he couldn't sleep at night. Moonlighting at the garage was an easy job for him because of the hours. "Howdy, Dwayne. Coming in late, huh?"

"Yeah, Fred. Me and Donna Sue went out to the Roadhouse to have some fun."

"Me and my old lady ain't never been there," the watchman said in an Oklahoma drawl. "We get our kicks at Western Danceland."

"You'd best be careful out there," Dwayne cautioned him.

"We always stay in our booth when a brawl brakes out," Fred said, pressing the button that raised the rail barrier. "We don't do no dancing 'til all the trouble is dealt with."

"Good idea," Dwayne said. He drove up to the second level and pulled into his rented space. He walked to the stairwell, going down to the ground floor. He gave Fred a wave as he left the building to go to the apartment house.

Over the years of being a military policeman and a private detective, Dwayne had developed an extra sense beyond the normal ones. At that exact moment gut feelings delivered a sudden punch to his psyche, giving a distinct warning signal.

He went past some tall shrubbery that lined the sidewalk, then ducked behind a thick oak tree and waited. Sure enough a man obviously following him appeared. Dwayne stepped out and grabbed the guy, viciously whirling him around and pushing him up against the tree.

"Anything I can do for you, pal?"

Another individual suddenly appeared out of the gloom. Dwayne shoved the first guy between himself and the other man. He drove the heel of his hand into the guy's face, making him stumble back. The second guy stepped in and managed to throw a punch at Dwayne, but only grazed him. Dwayne moved backward to get a little more room, but first guy was on his feet and he grabbed second guy. Both hurried off, breaking into a run. That was when Dwayne realized that they didn't want to pick a fight with him. They had only been keeping tabs on him.

Dwayne decided to keep the confrontation to himself. If he told Donna Sue about the incident she would get upset and worried. But all his instincts told him this could be the start of some rather disturbing difficulties. He couldn't deny it was time to let her in on the complete situation.

When he got back to the apartment Donna Sue was waiting for him with some wine for her and tumbler of Jack Daniels Sour Mash Whiskey for him. He took the glass and downed the liquor in a couple of gulps.

"Wow!" Donna Sue exclaimed with a giggle. "You

must've been looking forward to that all through the evening."

"We got to talk. I want to level with you about something. Something important."

She was still amused. "It better not be about another woman, buster."

"It ain't...isn't...about another woman."

Now she knew he was profoundly serious about something. "All right, Dwayne. Let's sit down. But first let me refresh your drink."

Dwayne took the second glass of the whiskey, and they sat down side-by-side on the sofa. "The first thing I want to tell you is to not fly off the handle right off the bat. Okay?"

"All right."

"I'm gonna start from the very beginning so I may be repeating myself to you, okay?"

"Certainly, Dwayne."

"When I got the job that paid me two hunnerd dollars a week, Pete Van Dyke told me it was all legal. It involved art work that was owned and traded around by a bunch of rich guys."

"So far, so good."

"The art would be sent to me and I would store it at a place here in Wichita. If a deal had been made, I would mail it to an address given me." He paused and took a deep swallow of whiskey. "Then I got called to go to Steve Williams office. He's the F.B.I. agent I deal with."

"I am familiar with Mister Williams."

"The art I was working with was stolen goods."

"*Goddamn it to hell, Dwayne!*"

"You're forgetting you promised not to get mad at me."

"I wasn't mad at you, Dwayne. I was just upset by

what seems to be happening."

"It was stolen from Jews in Europe," Dwayne said. "And Williams didn't know I had anything to do with it."

From that point on he revealed the entire episode and the fact that somebody important in Europe had discovered the art was in Wichita and he'd been hired to find it.

That gave Donna Sue a wonderful feeling of relief. "Then all you have to do is give it to them."

He hesitated. "Well...I didn't exactly tell them I knew where it was. I've been acting like I was looking for the stuff. Pete Van Dyke and I go back a long way. All the way back to the war and dealing in the German black market. And there was another thing we did, too. All I'll tell you is that it involved military scrip."

"Was it illegal?"

"Yes."

"*Goddamn it to hell, Dwayne!*"

"There's also another guy involved in that conspiracy. He's English and if him and Pete Van Dyke get arrested, they'll send me over. They could get reduced sentences for doing it."

"No problem, Dwayne. Then *you* send *them* over!"

"I'd still get a jail sentence and lose my private investigator license."

"Oh, Dwayne! What in hell are we gonna do?"

"The first thing I'm gonna do is get them tubes of paintings out of the vault rental joint and hide 'em."

"Hide them? I don't understand."

"Well, since they're worth millions, I think I just might be able to use 'em for a bargaining chip."

"Please, Dwayne, don't do anything that will get us into more trouble."

"Are you kidding? We're in as much trouble as we can possibly be already."

CHAPTER 35

Dwayne's plan for concealing the paintings began with a purchase of a 12 x 20 heavy canvas tarpaulin. He made the buy on a Wednesday afternoon, then drove over to Secure Vault Rentals to remove the paintings. Choosing that day was necessary because of where he planned to hide the art. That would be in the barn on his friend Tommy Brady's farm without the guy knowing about it. That decision was difficult for him since it would mean placing a good friend in a dangerous situation. But Dwayne had no other options.

The reason for him having to go on that particular day of the week and time, was that on Wednesday evenings, Tommy went into the town of Augusta to attend services at the local Methodist church. This would give Dwayne plenty of time to conceal the paintings while his pal was gone from the farm.

WHEN DWAYNE ARRIVED AT SECURE VAULT Rentals at six p.m., the manager Lawrence Gorcey was at the front counter. Dwayne asked to go to the strongbox he and Pete Van Dyke had rented.

"Certainly," Gorcey said. "We can take care of that right away."

"I'll need a cart to get the stuff out to my car."

Gorcey got one of the carts next to the wall, and escorted Dwayne to the storage area. After the two went through the usual procedure of providing the shamus access to the vault, the manager left Dwayne to his business.

Dwayne quickly opened the strongbox where a dozen cardboard tubes that ranged in length from two to four feet were stored. After placing them on the cart, he buzzed for Gorcey. The vault was relocked by the manager, then Dwayne wheeled the paintings out to the station wagon. Gorcey went with him to return the cart to the building.

With that done, he headed for Kellogg Street that was U.S. Highway 54 in Wichita. Dwayne drove east toward Augusta, then turned off and followed a road that led him close to Tommy Brady's farm. He parked and waited, keeping an eye on the crossroad a quarter of a mile ahead.

Tommy was a widower who had served in the Wichita Salvation Army with his wife Margie. After they retired, Tommy and Margie went to live on her parents' farm. When Margie died, Tommy remained on the property renting out fields to various farmers. During the ensuing years he had also helped Dwayne on a couple of capers.

Dwayne only had to wait twenty minutes before he sighted Tommy's blue pickup truck go through the intersection toward Augusta. The shamus immediately started up his own vehicle and headed up to the intersection. He turned in the opposite direction Tommy had gone, then steered the station wagon onto the short road up to the barn. He didn't have to worry about tire tracks since this was where tractors and trucks crossed when heading for the fields.

The first thing Dwayne did was to pull out the tarpaulin. He had rolled it up to make it easier to carry. After slinging it over his shoulder, he went inside the barn to a ladder attached to the wall. He climbed up to the loft and deposited the canvas cover on the floor, then went back down to the station wagon to get the cardboard tubes.

It took Dwayne fifteen minutes to get all twelve of the containers up to the loft. After laying the tubes on the tarpaulin, he folded the canvas over them, weighing it down with some lumber that had been stacked against the wall. The shamus went back down the ladder to the dirt floor. After closing the barn doors, he got into the station wagon and headed back for Wichita.

He was glad about getting the tubes hidden in the barn, but was still fretful about having to put Tommy Brady in such precarious circumstances.

———

DWAYNE'S TASK THE FOLLOWING DAY WAS TO put the German Jew David Arnsteiner under surveillance. He did not like the guy. Arnsteiner seemed to mistrust him and during the meetings in Steve Williams' office, he always questioned every statement that Dwayne made in his oral reports. However, the shamus had to admit to himself that he was pulling the wool over everyone's eyes since he was not really searching out the paintings.

Now he sat in the station wagon on Nineteenth Street, gazing toward the safehouse. He had some good concealment due to a large elm tree as well as the fences and shrubs that abounded in the neighborhood. Arnsteiner had never seen the Nash vehicle, but Dwayne was taking no chances.

After an hour Arnsteiner appeared, turning to walk away from Dwayne's location. The shamus could tell the guy wasn't just taking a casual stroll from the way he strode down the street. Dwayne pulled away from the curb and rolled along slowly, keeping an eye on the subject of the surveillance.

His quarry continued to a bus stop in a shopping area. Dwayne wondered why the Zionist would be taking a bus until an old Ford Sedan pulled up. Arnsteiner got in the auto and away they went, but Dwayne managed to get the license number. With that accomplished, he made a U-turn to go downtown.

———

WHEN HE ARRIVED BACK AT THE OFFICE, HE walked past Donna Sue. "I gotta make a phone call to the DMV."

She got to her feet and followed him to his desk. "What's going on?"

"I tailed Arnsteiner from the safehouse to a bus stop. But it was an old Ford that picked him up instead. The guy isn't supposed to know anybody in Wichita." He grabbed the telephone handset and dialed the number to the motor vehicle department. It didn't take long to get the information he sought. He looked over at Donna Sue. "The owner of the car is Donny Epstein. That's a Jewish name so I bet there's an organization here that's dealing with this same caper."

Donna Sue was curious. "Is 'Donny' a Jewish name?"

"I don't know, but that's what it sounded like. Donny. But Epstein is a Hebrew for sure. There was a guy I knew in the army with that name and he was Jewish."

The phone rang and Donna Sue responded with her usual greeting of, "Hello. Wheeler Detective Agency. Where may I direct your call?" She listened for a half minute then gave the handset to Dwayne. "It's Pete Van Dyke."

"Uh oh!" Dwayne cleared his throat. "Hello, Pete."

"*Where the fuck are those paintings, Dwayne?*"

"I'm not saying. But don't worry about it. They're safe and well concealed. Wait a minute. You must be in Wichita, right?"

"That's exactly where I am. At the Riverview Hotel. I went over to Secure Vault Rentals and there wasn't a thing in our strongbox. The manager said you showed up and took some articles out of it. What the hell are your intentions?"

"I think we should have a nice quite conversation regarding this situation, Pete. Is Sybil with you?"

"Yeah."

"Okay. I'll bring Donna Sue over with me and we can have one of those room service meals. How about tonight around seven?"

Pete seemed to calm down. "That's fine. And we have another problem to discuss. Nigel has disappeared. Nobody knows where he is. I'm thinking he got bumped off by some nasty individuals who want to know where the paintings are. This puts you and me in deep shit."

"You're right. We'll see you at seven." He hung up and

nodded to Donna Sue. "We're gonna have dinner with the Van Dykes at the Riverview Hotel."

Donna Sue was pleased. "I can wear that cocktail dress I bought last week."

"Forget it. The meal will be brought up by room service."

CHAPTER 36

Dwayne and Donna Sue stepped out of the elevator onto the Riverside Hotel's second floor. The shamus glanced over at his sweetheart. "Brace yourself. Pete is really pissed off about me hiding the loot."

"I just hope there isn't going to be a big scene between you two," she cautioned as they walked down the hall to Suite 206. "I'm hoping for a delicious meal with lots of entertaining conversation."

"Don't count on it."

They reached the door and Dwayne knocked. The summons was answered by Sybil who showed them a friendly smile. "Hi, you two. Come on in."

They walked into the suite and Dwayne noticed Pete sitting glumly in one corner of the sofa with a half filled glass of scotch-on-the-rocks at his elbow. Pete looked daggers at the two guests without uttering a word.

Sybil showed a cheerful disposition. "By the way, I have a surprise for you, Dwayne."

"Really? Orange Crush I bet."

"Better than that. Jack Daniels Sour Mash Whiskey. I

sent a hotel bellboy down to the corner liquor store and he checked out all the Jack Daniels' offerings until finding the right one."

"The guy hit the nail on the head!" Dwayne said with a big grin. He looked at Pete again, then swung his eyes back to Sybil. "I could use a tumbler of that goodness."

Sybil tended to the chore, then poured a couple of glasses of chardonnay for her and Donna Sue. With that done, she motioned the other woman to come with her across the room to a couple of easy chairs by the window. They settled down to sip the wine and observe their men.

Donna Sue wasn't sure about what was going on. "Is it all right for us gals to be here?"

"Certainly," Sybil assured her. "Both of us are in this as deep as they are."

Dwayne sat down on the far end of the sofa, glancing at Pete without saying a word as he waited for the dam to break. His ex-commanding officer took a swallow of the scotch then said, "Where's that fucking artwork, Dwayne?"

"In a safe place. Don't worry about it."

"Well goddamn it! I *am* worried about it. Now where's that fucking artwork?"

"I'll let you know when the time is right."

Pete growled, "The time is right this very fucking instant. Now you goddamn well better open up or it's gonna get real rowdy in here."

Sybil spoke up. "Take it easy, Pete."

Donna Sue joined in. "You, too, Dwayne."

Pete's temper didn't lessen. "Just what the hell are you doing here if you don't want to tell me what you're up to?"

"I never said I wouldn't tell you eventually. But we got some other things to discuss first."

"Such as?"

"Such as where the hell is Nigel Hawthorne?" Dwayne inquired. "You're the guy that can get ahold of him."

Pete calmed down at the mention of their English mentor. "Okay. Let me restart this session. I have no idea where Nigel is. I have several ways to get to him, but none have worked. The people I managed to speak to were surprised to hear the guy had disappeared. That has never happened before to his colleagues or customers."

"D'you think he's been knocked off?"

"I don't know," Pete admitted. "He might have tried to pull a double cross on those *SS* guys and got himself shot. I'm worried about that as well as the fact you've hidden away those paintings. None of this bullshit is doing my mood any good."

Dwayne drained his tumbler and stood up. "Let me freshen that drink of yours. Scotch, right? And I'll see how Jack Daniels is doing." He took care of the two libations, then returned and sat down again. "Pete, I think we're left out in the cold."

Pete gazed thoughtfully at him for about five seconds, licking his lips thoughtfully. "Maybe you're right. Maybe we're stuck with a couple of million dollars of old masterpieces."

Dwayne shook his head. "No, we're not. I have a fool-proof way to get rid of them and make some money, too. The fact the paintings were sent here to Wichita is well-known by the F.B.I. and the Zionist organization I mentioned when you called the last time."

Pete's face paled. "Do they know about you?"

Dwayne grinned and nodded his head. "Right. But they don't know it's me who has been receiving the goods. And they hired me to find whoever it might be."

"Well!" Pete exclaimed, brightening up. "Now this is a new and fresh development! Your reputation as a private eye is such that they figure you can dig out who is squirreling the art away. Right?"

"Yeah. I've been putting them off, making phony reports about investigating my contacts around Wichita. But now that's gotten more complicated. There's more Jewish guys involved in this than I first knew about. A couple were following me one night from the parking garage where I keep my station wagon. I surprised 'em and grabbed one. The other guy came up and pulled his buddy away. They didn't fight, but lit out for parts unknown."

"I see. That means they were just keeping tabs on you."

"And there's a third Jewish guy by the name of David Arnsteiner. He's been staying at an F.B.I. safehouse, but he's met another Zionist who lives in Wichita. At least his car has Kansas plates. His name is Donny Epstein and he's obviously been here quite awhile."

"Man!" Pete exclaimed. "We are really outnumbered."

Sybil was alarmed. "Is this getting dangerous?"

Donna Sue was also upset. "I don't like the sound of what's going on at all."

Pete shrugged, then glanced back at the shamus. "Hey, you have a twinkle in your eye, Dwayne. That generally means you've got a good idea."

"It's one I've had all along and the reason why I hid the paintings."

"Don't keep us in suspense!" Donna Sue demanded.

"Okay. I will go to the F.B.I. safehouse where Arnsteiner is staying. I'll wait 'til he goes out for a walk and follow him down the street. When I catch up to him, I'll honk and pull up to the curb."

Pete grinned. "You're gonna offer the guy a ride, huh?"

"Right. And when he gets in my car, I'm gonna tell him I can get the paintings, but I don't want the F.B.I. to know about it."

"Won't that make him suspicious?"

Dwayne shook his head. "I'm gonna tell him my so-called secret contact wants a cool fifty thousand bucks for the art."

"But what are you gonna tell the F.B.I. after the Jews leave Wichita?"

"I'll tell 'em I don't know nothing—*anything* —about 'em."

Sybil didn't like the amount. "But those paintings are worth at least a couple of million."

"That'd be a big bundle of cash to deal with," Dwayne said. "And it would look suspicious if anyone could produce that much dough on short notice."

"Right," Pete agreed. "That fictitious guy wouldn't have that much money invested in them."

"Here's another reason to let them Jews disappear," Dwayne said. "I want 'em to get the hell out of Wichita as quick as they can. And I'm sure they're gonna want to do just that. If they hang around, the F.B.I. is gonna haul the whole bunch in and sweat a lot of information out of 'em."

Pete had another point to make. "The Jews will want to see some evidence we can produce the stuff before they give us that much money."

"You're right. I'll get one of the tubes to show them before the deal goes down. That will leave eleven more hidden away."

"You'd better be careful about being tailed," Pete cautioned him.

"Nobody is gonna be able to follow me to the spot without standing out like a black cat on a white blanket. I can take care of that task late next Wednesday."

"Why wait that long?" Pete asked.

"It's the only way. That's all I'll say."

Donna Sue was uneasy about the fact that the F.B.I. was going to be left in the dark, but she decided not to mention any apprehension on her part except to say, "Make sure you open the rest of the tubes before you deliver them to make sure the artwork is inside."

Sybil reached over and patted Donna Sue's hand. "That's an excellent suggestion, dear."

"I've already checked that out," Dwayne assured them. He looked over at Pete. "Do you think it's time to call down for room service?"

"There's the menu on top of the radio."

CHAPTER 37

Yitzhak Cohen sat at an outside table in front of the tavern on *Ahorne Strasse*. This was the usual place for officers of the Zionist organization to meet with the agent Mordecai Hod. He had called Cohen at the Bureau of Property Recovery stating he would like to get together for a pleasant chat to catch up on things. Since it had been recently discovered that the telephones in West Germany had been interfered with by Russian NKVD agents, that mode of communication was no longer safe for classified discussions.

Cohen caught sight of Mordecai approaching and signaled to the waiter to bring another beer to the table. When the agent/concierge arrived, he sat down and waited to be served. "Hello, Yitzhak. How have you been, *mein Freund*?"

"Fine, *danke*. I am so happy you called."

Mordecai smiled. "I have some free time this morning, so I said to myself, 'I have not seen Yitzhak in a while. I must have a chat with him to find out how things are going for him.'"

The waiter appeared and wordlessly sat the stein on the table, then returned to the interior of the tavern. Mordecai took a sip of beer then leaned forward and whispered, "Nigel Hawthorne has disappeared. And that includes his girlfriend Lale."

Cohen was concerned. "How long have they been gone?"

Mordecai shrugged. "I have no idea. My wife Ester told me she had not seen them for a few days. So I went up to their apartment and knocked as if to make an inquiry on their plumbing. After receiving no response, I used my passkey to open the door. Everything looked normal at first, but when I went through the flat I could see that the only belongings left were nondescript and unimportant."

"Did you not see them leave, carrying luggage?"

Mordecai shrugged. "I would not be able to observe them if they came down in the elevator and went out the side door of the building. That area is not visible from my concierge station. The last time I saw them was when they returned from an evening out. We had a brief conversation and they left me and went toward the elevators. They could have snuck away any time after that incident."

"This is serious," Cohen said, wishing David Arnsteiner was present. "It could mean that the *SS*-men at the *Wolflager* may be planning a transfer of their operations."

"I thought of that, too. If we lose track of them, it might take months to find out where they went. You have to make the right choice as to the best way to handle this predicament. And you must do so without delay."

Cohen showed a wry grin. "It is like the Americans say. I am between a rock and the hard place. Or something like that."

At that point they fell into some idle talk until Mordecai finished his beer. He stood up and shook hands with Cohen, then walked back up the street in the direction he had come from.

Cohen had already figured out what he must do in these new and very alarming circumstances. And the best place to begin the investigation would be a visit to Lieutenant Colonel Roger Kobelski.

———

DWAYNE WHEELER SAT IN HIS NASH STATION wagon on 19th Street at a good site to keep watch on the F.B.I.'s safehouse. Dwayne had a cardboard tube pushed between the driver's side door and seat. The evening before, he had snuck back into Tommy Brady's barn and taken it out with him. He was still keeping that secret from Pete.

An impatient half hour passed before Dwayne spotted David Arnsteiner leaving the residence. The shamus started the engine, pulled out from the curb and drove slowly down the street until catching up with the German Jew.

He pulled up to the curb. "Arnsteiner!"

The man turned abruptly and looked at the car, then noticed that Dwayne was driving. He stopped. "Yes?"

Dwayne leaned over. "I have something important to talk to you about."

Arnsteiner didn't hesitate to get into the vehicle. "I hope you have some good news for me, Mister Wheeler."

"I don't think you'll be disappointed."

They drove over to Riverside Park to a deserted picnic area. After parking, Dwayne carried the cardboard tube as they walked to a nearby table and sat down. Dwayne wasted no time or words in speaking to Arnsteiner. "I can get the missing paintings for you."

"I see. And where does the F.B.I. fit in here?"

"Fuck the F.B.I.," Dwayne replied. "Now listen up. I'm talking about all the artwork. My contact who has it wants fifty thousand dollars."

Arnsteiner was skeptical. "Can you trust this person?"

"Of course. He is an old acquaintance of mine. Completely reliable. And he has stated, 'No money. No pictures.' Get it?" He paused. "He wants old bills that have been in circulation for awhile. And I'm warning you, don't do any hemming and hawing or other bargaining bullshit. I know you have a contact here. Name of Donny Epstein. There's also been a coupla guys that tailed me. I dealt with 'em in my own charming way."

"Yes. I know about that."

"And *we* know you can get the big bucks we need to close the deal," Dwayne stated, rolling the cardboard tube across the table. Arnsteiner picked it up and pulled the top off the device. He extracted the canvases and spread them out. He gasped audibly, as he recognized the paintings stolen from of his house in Sommerfeld.

Dwayne looked sharply at him. "What's the matter? You got some problem with them pictures."

Arnsteiner caught his breath. "Uh...no. They are obviously authentic. I have no doubt about that."

Dwayne asked, "Then you're satisfied these are the real McCoy, right?"

"Yes."

The shamus took the paintings and returned them to the tube while speaking to Arnsteiner. "So! You do what you gotta do to raise the fifty grand and I'll wait. And you better hurry. My contact is anxious to be rid of the merchandise. Any long delays and he'll go somewhere else."

"I understand."

"Okay. Can I give you a ride someplace?"

Arnsteiner shook his head. "No, thank you. I shall take a little stroll around the neighborhood. Then I will make a phone call." He looked over at Dwayne. "Thank you very much."

"You're welcome very much," Dwayne replied. He walked away with the paintings, leaving Arnsteiner sitting at the picnic table.

CHAPTER 38

A dozen military intelligence representatives from the American, British and French armies sat around a table in a special soundproofed conference room. This chamber was located in the basement of the Allied Criminal Investigation Division Headquarters. This was in the West German capital city of Bonn where the three powers coordinated their mutual efforts in the hodgepodge of criminal and espionage activities that was concentrated throughout postwar Europe.

The host of that particular day's activities was Lieutenant Colonel Roger Kobelski of the U.S. Army. He was accompanied by Yitzhak Cohen who had prepared four large packets of information and maps for himself, Kobelski, and the British and French representatives. Those bundles contained important intelligence provided over the last two years by the young German Herbert Hock who delivered information piecemeal to the Displaced Persons Registration Office.

The meeting began with Kobelski introducing Cohen to the British and French officers. Cohen gave a brief but complete introduction about the *Wolflager* and the not-to-be-identified informant that had penetrated the group of ex-*Waffen-SS* Nazis. "This mole is under our protection," Cohen informed them. "And he is going to remain a secret."

Kobelski remarked, "I believe we can all honor that request."

"Excellent, gentlemen," Cohen said. Then he launched into a description of the *SS* men's mission, operations and personnel as well as the location of the headquarters. Cohen also readily admitted that the original plans of the Zionists was for a Jewish fighting group to make a raid on the *Wolflager*. However, certain circumstances had arisen that made that impractical. Therefore, he had contacted Lieutenant Colonel Kobelski about utilizing the Allied armies occupying West Germany.

At that point Kobelski took over, explaining that the general staffs of the Allied military forces had approved making an attack on the neo-Nazis. It was also decided to include the West German police in the operation. This was to publicize that West Germany was now being denazified and willing to punish German citizens who had committed war crimes.

At that point, Cohen spoke up again, identifying the present West German police commissioner Werner Ullmann as actually being a former *Allgemeine-SS* member who served the *Wolflager*. During the war he had conducted brutal interrogations of special prisoners as a clandestine member of the *Gestapo;* the spoken acronym of *Geheime Staatspolizei*, i.e. the State Secret Police.

Thus began an intense question-and-answer conference that went on for two hours before all four men were satisfied of the intelligence side of dealing with the *Waffen-SS* veterans. They were confident of being able to take accurate, up-to-date briefings back to their respective headquarters to augment the final issue of operation orders.

Just before adjourning the meeting, Roger Kobelski informed them that a joint force of American, British and French officers along with West German policemen was already working on the tactical angle for the attack on the *Wolflager* by using a sand table of the target's location. This piece of equipment had been constructed from aerial photos made secretly by U.S. Army Air Force planes flying over the site at high altitudes.

The date of the assault on the *Wolflager* was kept even from Kobelski. The U.S. Army's operations staff also did not inform the local F.B.I. office.

———

THE TRANSFER OF THE PAINTINGS TOOK PLACE IN the morning at the same spot in Riverside Park where Dwayne had revealed the tube with the five pieces of art. David Arnsteiner had wanted Dani Epstein to be present, but Dwayne would only allow the other Jew to park his car at the curb and wait for Arnsteiner to finalize the deal with the American.

"Let's see the dough," Dwayne said. He had placed all twelve cardboard tubes on the ground by his feet.

Arnsteiner set a large attaché case he'd brought with him on the picnic table. He opened it and pulled out ten packets of $5,000 each. Dwayne thumbed through each one, noting all were filled with worn bills. With that done he stepped back, pointing to the tubes. "Check 'em out, Arnsteiner."

Now Arnsteiner picked up the containers one by one, removing each individual painting. He examined and counted them, noting there was a grand total of thirty-six masterpieces.

"Good enough," he pronounced.

"Nice doing business with you," Dwayne said. He put the money in his briefcase, then got to his feet. "Good luck with that Israel deal you're working on." He passed Dani Epstein heading toward Arnsteiner to help him carry the paintings to his car.

CHAPTER 39

Two days after the transfer of artwork, Dwayne was called to go upstairs to the F.B.I. office. When he arrived, he noted the very critical expression on secretary Ruth Henderson's face. She was blunt, saying, "Mister Williams said you are to report to him the moment you arrived."

"Report?" Dwayne asked, displaying a wide-eyed look of innocent surprise. "Whatever for?"

Miss Henderson ignored the question.

Dwayne stepped inside and sat down on a chair in front of Steve Williams' desk. Agent Larry Tomlinson was standing off to the side. He seemed as unhappy and disapproving as Miss Henderson.

Dwayne showed a cheerful demeanor. "What's going on, guys?"

Williams spoke through clenched teeth. "David Arnsteiner has disappeared. Do you know anything about it?"

"I thought he was staying in the safehouse."

Tomlinson stated, "He has disappeared from that residence."

Dwayne went into his well-played act of surprise. "Jesus! That was unexpected, wasn't it? Where the hell do you think he went? And why?"

Williams leaned back in his chair. "The F.B.I. thinks you know about this situation and perhaps played an active part in the guy's disappearance."

"The F.B.I. thinks *I* know about this? The whole fucking F.B.I.? Even J. Edgar Hoover?"

Tomlinson was livid. "Don't play smart with us, Wheeler!"

"I ain't playing smart. I'm playing sarcastic."

Williams wanted information and he wanted it fast. "The guy was here in Wichita all by his lonesome. In order to sneak away, he'd need outside help."

"Why would I help him?"

Tomlinson sat on the edge of the desk and leaned toward the shamus. "To give him the hidden artwork that your secret confederate passed on to you."

"Confederate? What is this, the Civil War?" Dwayne said with a chuckle.

Tomlinson was not amused. "A confederate is an accomplice."

"I was making a joke."

Williams lit a cigarette and eyed Dwayne for a full ten seconds, trying to judge the private eye's truthfulness. "We know about Dani Epstein."

Oh, shit! Dwayne thought. "Who the hell is Epstein?"

Tomlinson yelled, "You know goddamn well who the guy is!"

"No I don't!" Dwayne yelled back. He was now extremely agitated and nervous. He decided to bluff it out.

"He sounds like he's important. His name is Jewish, ain't it? So call him in and wring him out."

"We can't," Williams admitted. "He's got diplomatic immunity. Although the state of Israel is not yet established, it's already recognized by the American Government. It seems this Epstein guy is some kind of envoy."

Dwayne was relieved and decided to appear cooperative. "Well, fellahs, it looks like we're all up that familiar ol' creek without a paddle. That Israel nation was a few steps ahead of us, right?"

Tomlinson was still angry but Williams knew they were at a dead end. "Thanks for coming in, Dwayne."

He stood up. "You're welcome. Give me a call when I can come back and pick up my check for the services I rendered to J. Edgar Hoover."

CHAPTER 40

Pete and Sybil Van Dyke left Wichita to return to New York. They had their twenty-five thousand cut of the art deal stashed in the lining of Sybil's mink coat. After a short conversation with Dwayne just before beginning the trip, Pete decided it was in both their interests if he conducted an investigation on his own to find out what happened to Nigel Hawthorne.

Dwayne and Donna Sue stuck their share of the payment for the art in the closet hiding place. That money, as always, would be eased into their personal and business bank accounts over a long period of time. With that done, they settled back into the routine of running the detective agency and planning its further expansion.

——

THE ATTACK ON THE *WOLFLAGER* BY THE combined Allied military and police units began in the early morning moments before the sun began to rise above the forest trees. Using maps furnished by Yitzhak

Cohen, they first took down the manned guard stations within the wooded area. The sentries were handcuffed and taken back to waiting trucks. With that done, they set up machine guns and mortars at the edge of the tree line. These powerful weapons would support a West German police squad and an infantry platoon each from the American, British and French armies when the order to attack was issued.

An officer of the West German police took a hand-held loud speaker and informed the *SS* men inside that they were surrounded. He advised them that they had fifteen minutes to present themselves outside the building with their hands up.

Five minutes passed, then Bruno Schlagger and two more men appeared on the porch. They had a white sheet and waved it back and forth to indicate they wanted a parley. The policeman with the loud speaker ordered them to walk to the center of the open field.

Lieutenant Colonel Roger Kobelski along a British officer, French officer and German policeman for a translator walked out to meet the trio of *Waffen-SS* men. A conference began in which Schlagger told them they would surrender, but needed at least a half hour to make an appearance.

This did not suit Kobelski. He ordered the translator to tell them they had fifteen minutes to give up. He pointed to the tree line. "There are a hundred troops with machine guns, mortars and rifles. If you do not come out, all that firepower is going to be coming down on you."

Schlagger promised they would obey, then he and his buddies double-timed back to the house. The Allied officers watched them.

"I don't trust the bastards," Kobelski growled.

The British officer grinned. "They'll obey our terms,

Colonel. They are former elite German soldiers who have already known a devastating defeat. They had survived that catastrophe. The strength of our group out here indicates they would die for another failed cause if they engaged us in combat. It's true the *SS-men* face prison sentences, but the day will come when they will be released back into West German society."

Within twelve minutes, thirty men came out with their hands on top of their heads. After they were taken into custody a detachment of American M.P.s went inside the building to sweep the interior. They found two suicides. Manfred von Leipinger and Franz Taubert each with self-inflicted shots fired into their temples using German Luger nine-millimeter pistols laid face-down on their respective desks.

————

EARLY ONE EVENING THERE WAS A KNOCK ON THE door of the Hock house in Sommerfeld. Both Herbert and his father went to see who had come visiting. When the elder Hock opened the door, Herbert saw a Jewish man he had met during visits to the Displaced Persons Registration Office. The visitor handed a canvas bag to Herbert's father, saying, "There is enough money here for you to rebuild your printing business that was shelled during the war."

After handing over the cash, the man turned and walked down the street. "Wait!" *Herr* Hock shouted. "What is—"

Herbert grasped his father's arm, saying, "Let him go, *Vater*. It is all legal and above board. Believe me."

Herr Hock looked at his son, asking, "Do you know about this?"

"I know everything about it, *Vater.*"

Hock embraced Herbert and kissed him on the cheek, then turned toward the kitchen where his wife was. "Elsa! You will never believe what just happened!"

———

DWAYNE WHEELER AND DONNA SUE CONNORS became man-and-wife in the Sedgwick County court-house a week following the closing of the art caper. There were a dozen people attending the late afternoon cere-mony. These well wishers were the four barbers from the OK Barbershop, three bookies, a trio of ex-bootleggers and their wives along with Mr. and Mrs. A.J. Kessler. Also present was Tommy Brady who was not aware that Dwayne had hidden millions of dollars' worth of master-piece paintings in his barn loft.

After the wedding, the group drove up to the Stock-yards Hotel Restaurant for steak dinners. Dwayne and Donna Sue hosted the event in the establishment's banquet room.

———

IT WAS NINE O'CLOCK IN THE EVENING WHEN THE wedding festivities finally came to an end. Everyone left the dining hall and went outside to their cars. Dwayne and Donna made their goodbyes and accepted the best wishes of their guests before everyone drove away.

Dwayne and Donna Sue got into the Nash and headed south on Broadway to their apartment. After a few minutes of driving, Dwayne spoke up. "I wonder what's waiting for us down the road of life."

Donna Sue gave him a determined look. "There had

better not be any more crooked capers. So you just be careful!"

"Okay."

"I mean it, Dwayne Wheeler!"

He made no reply.

A Look At Book 5:

Wichita Nimrod

1940s Wichita, Kansas

When Private Detective Dwayne Wheeler returns from his honeymoon, he receives an unexpected call from Agent Harry Philbin of the Kansas Bureau of Investigation. With the KBI overloaded by narcotics crimes, Philbin offers Dwayne a temporary position—investigate several mysterious farmhouse burglaries.

Accepting the job, Dwayne discovers that the farmers have never seen fit to lock their front doors. Yet...this is the first time that criminals have struck—every break-in happening on Sunday morning while each victim is busy attending church. To make matters worse, a racket in which stolen cars are being stripped down is uncovered, and Dwayne is tasked with finding the unknown merchants.

But when a murder blasts on the scene, Dwayne's world is turned upside down. Will his KBI-assigned cases take a back seat... Or will he use his devastation as ammunition to tie up loose ends once and for all?

Wichita Nimrod is book five in a historical private eye series that follows Dwayne Wheeler—a tough and hardboiled detective.

AVAILABLE NOVEMBER 2022

About the Author

Patrick Andrews was born an Army Brat on January 14, 1936—his sister's arrival just two years later. His father was a paratrooper in the 82nd Airborne Division during World War II. His mother was a good army officer's wife, who, like several of her lady cousins, wrote short-stories and poems.

After the war, Patrick's father transferred into the Army Reserves, and they moved to Wichita, Kansas—where Patrick caught the scribbling bug. When Patrick got a job as a copy boy at the *Wichita Eagle* newspaper, he was ecstatic.

A few years later, Patrick got a yen to be a paratrooper. He enlisted in the Army and took basic training in Camp Chaffee, Arkansas, soon after being transferred to the 82nd Airborne Division in Fort Bragg. His career with the 82nd was rewarding—being promoted to sergeant and tasked with training cadets in West Point before retiring.

When Patrick read James Jones' *From Here to Eternity*, he appreciated the pride and struggling of soldiers. Soon after, he moved to San Diego, California and began writing and mailing manuscripts while working at a union typesetting company. He married and had one child, named William Patrick.

One pivotal night, Patrick was with a couple of his writing buddies, drinking scotch whiskey and playing at writing the *Sixgun Samurai* series. The next day, they drove up to Pinnacle Books in Los Angeles, where they walked out with a book deal. Patrick and his friends went on to write the series' twelve novels—which were also printed in the U.K. by Star Books, the paperback division of W.H. Allen & Co.

From then on, Patrick started writing and selling western, men's adventure, and military fiction. Years passed, and he had 24 published e-books with Piccadilly Publishing in the U.K.

Today, all six of Patrick's Wichita Detective books are getting another chance to see the light of day—with Rough Edges Press—and find refuge on a cozy shelf in Ocean Hills, California where Patrick and his beloved wife, Julie, live.